Seven and a Half Minutes

Seven and a Half Minutes

The Polo Diaries Book 3

Roxana Valea

Prologue

There are three types of people who play polo.

There are those who play from the head. You see them looking around the field with wrinkled foreheads and half-closed eyes. Calculating, imagining, visualizing, thinking. Thinking hard. They practice a lot, repeating the same movements over and over again. They obsess about the game before they play; they think hard during the game, trying to anticipate what's happening; and they can't stop thinking about it afterwards, analyzing the details, trying to remember and create a formula of all that went well, trying to eliminate all that went wrong. They are the thinkers.

Then there are those who play from the guts. Instinctual, passionate, visceral. They play from deep down inside, from the place where we all live and survive, deep in the belly, the place of our identity. They play to feel good, to look good, to make good all that went wrong before. They play with the fierce instinct of the survivor. They play for honor, for glamour, for recognition. They play hard, and they give it their all, as if polo were the one thing that would redeem them in their own eyes and in the eyes of all those around them. They are the feelers.

And then there are those who play from another place. Who don't think and don't feel, either. Who flow. Those who are so deeply immersed in the moment that it simply does not matter any longer what happens on the field, because the game, the horse, and the mallets have all melted and become one. They play from a place of infinite beauty, from a place of timeless joy. They play from the core of their beings, the same core that connects them to the horse, to the field, and to one another. They play as if this moment were everything. And in this place of timeless beauty, of deep connection to everything, of joy and flow, there's no space for either thought or feeling. They play from the heart.

This book is for them.

A Picture Does Not Say It All

JULY

A picture does not say it all. It's just an instance in time, frozen, and it lets the viewer fill in the blanks with imagination.

It does not talk about the hours, the hours on the field. The drives out of London, the traffic lights, the rush. And finally, on the highway, the one big question: Will I make it in time for tonight's chukkas?

It does not show the color of the wheat in the field next to where we train. How could it? Wheat has many colors. My favorite is the deep green of early spring, just as it comes out.

It does not tell of the taste of sweat at the end of the last chukka, when you rest your head against the horse, both of you out of breath and your sweat mixing together. The taste of it: sour and salty at the same time. And the heat rising from the horse, which remains still after you have dismounted, the heat rising from its body like a cloud rising to the sky.

The hours spent hitting the ball, missing the ball, getting angry at the ball, and riding the wave of frustration building inside as you shout the burning question: "Why? What must I do to hit this ball?"

"Hit more balls," comes the answer from the calm-faced rider behind. "Just hit more balls."

I hit more balls. I get angry with them, and I miss them. "Connect!" I hear the shout from behind. "Just connect with it!"

"How does one connect?" I wonder. I try sending love to the ball. It works as if by magic.

I hit balls under the rain and under the sun. I hit them when the ground has turned into a mud swamp after three weeks of constant rain, and they all burrow into the mud. I hit them when the ground is hard, so hard that every step of the horse vibrates to the very center of my brain. The wheat in the field next door has changed color. It's turning yellow now.

We hit more balls. He hits to me, and I hit to him, in silence, day after day. Tail! Open! Forward! Cut! Near side! I obey this young pro with a serious face, who doesn't smile but who plays polo like a god. I ride on and do just as he says.

"Please don't let them change your riding." I hear the pleading of my first polo coach, the guy who taught me everything I know about riding. I promised him silently I'd stick to my English half-seat, even if I'm now betraying him with the Argentines.

Sure enough, I hold still as my Argentine coach tries to tell me to move my legs forward into the saddle. "Sorry, no. English style," I say, and he gives up and we go back to hitting. Argentine and English: two different styles a world apart, although my two clubs are only twenty miles away from each other. I try to reconcile these two worlds. Slowly, painfully, and stretching far out of its comfort zone, my body is crafting its own style: ride like the English, hit like the Argentines. Both parties are unhappy, but I've never been very good with fitting into widely accepted models anyway. I hit more balls…

I get hooked by a 0-goal player. The pain in my forearm lasts two weeks. Then I get ridden off by another one, a far, far better player than me. I feel my left knee painfully locked behind his, with his horse just an inch in front of mine—just what he needs to get me out of play completely—and then he carries on, doesn't leave the lock to go play but enjoys his skill and his power and the show he's making of them both, keeping me locked there despite my struggle to free myself, despite my horse's heavy breathing and the anger that's rising fast in me. In front of my eyes, a paragraph from the *Blue Book* starts dancing: "The player shall not use his elbow, fist, stick, or whip to hit another player or his horse…" I didn't understand it when I first read it, but now I do. Now I fully understand why they needed to add that paragraph. But I don't hit, don't kick, and don't even swear. I just send him to hell silently in my mind.

The names of the horses I ride mix in my head with the names of the people I love. My favorite is a solid fifty-three-inch-stick light brown mare that looks like a thoroughbred. She's fast, and she's so stable that no matter how far I lean out of the saddle to hit that ball, I know I'll always manage to get back on her. She's hard in the mouth, though, and difficult to stop, and I know that riding her in a chukka will probably result in Morgan sticking two more of his acupuncture needles in my *latissimus dorsi* muscles.

He knows my body so well; Morgan, I mean. He follows my lower back pain as it travels to the centre of my back, then to my shoulder blades, where it decides to stay for a while. More acupuncture needles. More stretching, more of the bone-cracking and that worrying sound of ribs clicking under his chiropractic moves. Then the pain travels up my neck, down to my elbows, and eventually decides to leave my body.

For a few weeks now, I've not found it anywhere. "What's going on?" I ask him one Monday evening, our usual appointment time, as I lie down on his bench, his expert hands pulling and twisting and pressing my known trigger points.

"Nothing, it's gone." He smiles. "Your body has become like steel."

The picture cannot capture the nights either. The night that falls at the end of the game on a Wednesday evening. The silence of the fields after the sunset, the humming of the grooms as they untack and release the horses into the fields, the drive back to London with aching legs.

Forgot to wash my hands, so now my car smells of horse. Arrive back home late, too late for dinner, but that is replaced with a protein shake in the car, somewhere at the junction of the M4 and M24. Straight to bed. It's almost midnight, and tomorrow is another day.

"You have to feel your horse between your legs." I check his face, searching for signs of a double meaning, but, no, his face is straight. He talks polo, he breathes polo, he rides eight horses a day, and he is not in the mood for jokes. I hit more balls with my silent companion, and I feel he's right: my tired legs have already given in. I stick my knees in, drop my heels out, and try to imagine a fifty pound note that must not drop stuck somewhere between my knee and the saddle. It's a trick I picked up from a blond surfer turned pro polo player somewhere in Argentina. It works every time.

The guy in front of me swings his mallet into a backhand. It's supposed to be open, but the ball flies a few inches in front of my nose. Too close, far too close. I still play without a face guard. *Play positive*, I hear in my mind the words of another coach. *Play positive: don't think about the worst.*

No, I don't think, but I have seen what a ball in the face does to people. This thought is still with me when my team takes a penalty, and, as number one, I'm the one who's supposed to be in front of the goal defending it. For some reason I cannot bring myself to do it, standing there still on my horse, waiting for that small, hard ball to come to me at speed. I simply cannot do it. Better let one of the guys do it. The number two of my team swears in a whisper as he takes my place at the goalpost.

The picture does not capture the eternity of the seven and a half minutes. A place out of space, a time out of time. An eternity, a whole life that dances in front of your eyes while your mind has shut down. Seven and a half minutes where the mind has nothing to say: it cannot. Seven and a half minutes where the body takes over completely, totally, showing you it knows much more than you give it credit for. It turns before you have time to think about turning, it stops, it guesses where the ball is going, and it reaches out before you have any time to plan the shot. Seven and a half minutes where all you can do is dance, fly on the back of a horse, and together you become neither human nor animal. An eternity all packed into a seven-and-a-half-minute chukka.

And the picture does not show the handshake after the end of the last chukka either: the tired smiles, the heavy breathing, the togetherness of people and horses once again back from the battle—a memory as deep as mankind. And I even shake the hand of the guy who so successfully rode me off. My anger is gone, and nothing matters any longer, not even who won the game.

Only a picture, leaving the blanks to be filled by imagination. In the minds of my friends, that's sexy polo players, parties till dawn, champagne, and sparkling outfits. I let them believe this; everyone has the right to dream as they please. In the meantime, I go on with my own dream. With my brown boots on and a fifty-two-inch mallet, I jump into the saddle and take my horse towards the stick-and-ball field. And I wonder what color the wheat will be today.

But this story didn't start there with the horse and the mallet and the polo field. All this came much later. Long before I knew a polo chukka lasted for seven and a half minutes, and long before I ever shook hands with anyone on a horse, I was just a single girl lost in a big city, trying to follow the formula others had laid out for me: work hard, go out and party, find a man, and settle down.

This story started on a rainy late autumn evening under the neon lights of a night club in London…

Riding Boots

OCTOBER

I patiently wait for the next guy to take the empty seat in front of me, and once again I curse my decision to come here tonight. I can't believe I'm doing this. Speed dating. Am I really that desperate?

I'd been single for a while, it's true, and nothing had seemed to help me find Mr. Right. My life was a never-ending sequence of flat whites at Starbucks, work, journeys on the underground, home, sleep. And repeat. I badly craved some excitement, and I thought I'd have it and more if only I met Mr. Right. My friends told me to try online dating, but I didn't believe in search-engine matching technology. I'm rather old-fashioned; for me, a man is a flesh-and-bone being, not some heavily edited photo on the net. But the problem with the work–home routine is that there's little opportunity to meet this flesh-and-bone person who is neither your neighbor (already checked them all and found nobody suitable) nor a work colleague (same).

I had to try something else. So I did. I booked a ticket at this speed-dating event, and I was already starting to regret it.

Girls remain seated, one next to the other. There are about ten of us. Guys change chairs every five minutes when the organizer claps her hands. Each of us has a pen and a piece of paper, where we're supposed to rate the eligible bachelors who take turns introducing themselves.

I want to get out of here as soon as possible. Just a couple more guys, I tell myself. Let's do it. The man of my life might be the very next one; let's give him a chance.

The next guy takes the seat in front of me. I can't really see his face very well because of the dimmed lights. They should organize these events somewhere with better lighting. He talks a lot, but I lose him at the beginning of his introduction. I'm irritated to be there and irritated by my irritation. At least now that I'm here, let's make the best of it! I sigh and try hard to concentrate on what he's telling me. I catch only the end of his sentence:

"My favorite thing in life is watching TV, and I'm looking for a girlfriend to share this with," he says in a serious voice. I glance at him expecting to hear it was a joke but, no, unfortunately, he's serious. I maintain a blank face and don't volunteer an answer. I guess he understands I'm not the woman to make his dream come true. He moves on to the next seat and probably repeats the same sentence to the girl next to me. I don't know for sure, because, once again, I'm not listening. I'm just busy making sense of what I see in front of me. Someone else takes his seat, but it's not a potential eligible bachelor. It's a woman in her late fifties. Somewhat overweight, displaying a pair of huge breasts, and a dark red lipstick that makes her thick lips stand out even more.

What the hell? This is supposed to be a straight dating event!

But the woman watches me with serious eyes and gives me a little time to recover from the shock. She asks only one question:

"Are you tired of this?"

Yes, actually, I am. All of a sudden I feel really heavy. Like I want to lie under the table or anywhere I can just have a rest. I've always envied dogs. They can lie down wherever they happen to be, just because they feel like it. I wish I were a dog sometimes.

"Yes, I'm tired. But I want to meet someone," I say.

Someone. Isn't it funny how we say we want to meet *someone*? Not *the one*. Just someone. As if anyone would do. When you've been searching long enough, anyone halfway decent *would* do.

"I can help," she says laconically and hands me a business card. Then the organizer claps her hands, and she moves on to the girl next to me. Another man takes her seat now. I wonder how she does it. She must have paid a handsome fee to the organizer for this chance to pitch her services to overtired ladies pushing themselves to go on with a fierce determination to find *someone*.

The guy in front of me starts talking rapidly. He's only got five minutes, and he's determined not to waste them. But I don't hear, I don't even look at him. I stare at the card in my hand. It says:

Joan Gilbert—Love Coach

I call her because it's a week after my birthday, and I still can't figure out what present I want. I have a tradition of buying myself a birthday present every year, but this year I just can't think of anything. All I want is a boyfriend. But they don't sell boyfriends at any of the shops in downtown London, so I decide to call her instead and agree to pay her full exorbitant fee for a consultation.

All I hope is that she's got a magic bullet. Something that would lead me quickly and painlessly straight to *someone*. But five minutes into the conversation, I understand that she doesn't. All she can say is that it isn't about the man. It's about me.

I sigh. This is precisely what I was afraid of. She's now going to give me some New Age mumbo jumbo about how I have to find myself first.

"You mean I have to love myself first, right?"

I don't make any effort to hide the irony in my voice.

"Precisely," she says. "You can't love someone else until you love yourself."

"So how do I do that?" I ask, deciding to play this game. After all, I have paid for the full session already. I might as well keep talking to her, magic bullet or not.

"You connect with your passions," she replies.

My passions? I haven't had time to think about this. I'm not even sure what my passions are. All I do is work ten hours a day for a big company in downtown London, come home, order a takeaway for dinner, watch Netflix, and go to sleep. I go out on a Friday or Saturday evening, sometimes both. I hope to meet someone. I come back home after meeting no one and watch another Netflix movie to help me fall asleep. I wake up late with a hangover on Sunday and drag myself to the gym. Maybe I meet a girlfriend for a coffee. And then I start the week all over again.

"I have no passions," I tell her after a while.

"How about when you were a little girl? What did you like to do when you were twelve, for instance?"

I don't expect this question. A lot of time has passed since I was twelve.

"Ride horses," I say.

I've got no idea where this memory came from, but it's pretty vivid. I loved riding horses as a child.

"How long have you been riding?" she asks.

"A few years."

And then the rest of the memories come flooding back. The big, old black horse I learned to ride on, Samurai was his name. Patiently turning in a circle, held on a rope by my instructor. Then I was left to trot and canter on my own in a metal enclosure. The first fall, straight into the middle of a mud puddle. Having to lie about it to my parents for fear they wouldn't let me ride again. And the best birthday present I ever got from them: a pair of well-polished black riding boots when I turned fourteen. I rode for a few more years, and then I slowly lost it. Other things became more important. Things like getting a university degree, a boyfriend, and a new pair of heels.

"How about you do that again?" my love coach suggests.

"What, riding? How is that going to help me find a boyfriend?" I ask, unconvinced.

"It'll help you get in touch with your passion," she says. "And this is the first step towards anything else."

I don't remember much of what she said afterwards. Just filling time probably till the end of the session. I didn't believe finding my passion had anything to do with finding someone, but I remembered to fetch my old riding boots the next time I went to visit my parents. I took them down from the attic where they'd been stored for the last twenty-four years and brought them back with me to my London flat.

And now what? I ask myself contemplating the pair of worn-out black riding boots looking somewhat out of place in the middle of my living room. I'm no longer a girl of twelve; I'm a woman of thirty-eight. A single woman of thirty-eight, I should say.

And it's about time I found someone.

When Bentley Met Ziggy

JANUARY

The winter holidays come and go, and I find myself buried in the same routine: work, home, sleep. Repeat. I don't meet anyone. I don't do anything with my riding boots either.

And then, late in January, on a frozen winter morning, something magical happens on the streets of London: Bentley meets Ziggy. It is a chance encounter that might have lasted only a few seconds, and then nothing else would have happened, and I would never have played polo, and all these stories would not have existed. But fate decided differently. It was meant to be that Bentley and Ziggy were allowed to have a longer conversation, and that changed my life. Forever.

I wasn't there to witness this encounter, but Girlie, my friend, told me the details of the story many times, because what happened changed not only my life but hers as well.

Bentley went nose first and gently said hello. Bentley was a very well-behaved, sweet-looking cocker spaniel. Ziggy, on the other hand, looked like a greyhound that had come out of a tumble dryer, his fur running wild in all directions. While Bentley was the picture-perfect dog, Ziggy was a dog you would never forget once you met him.

As the dogs sniffed and socialized, Bentley's mum said hello to Ziggy's dad. Like the dogs, the owners were polar opposites. She was an elegant lady in her mid-thirties, living in a trendy London neighborhood, working as a manager for a well-respected multinational. She wore designer clothes, had impeccably manicured hands, and loved London's fine-dining scene. She was a work colleague of mine. I called her Girlie.

He, on the other hand, was an eccentric artist in his sixties. A heap of scruffy white hair matched the look of his dog. Usually dressed in worn-out jeans, he spent his time collecting art, walking his dog and… well, there was something else that took up most of his time and money. But Girlie didn't know any of this. She just pulled the collar of her winter jacket higher up to keep the cold away and gave the stranger a polite nod. They seemed to be neighbors, but they had never met before. And, because, in England, when two perfect strangers meet they usually talk about the weather, the dialogue went like this:

Neighbor: "A bit cold, isn't it?"

Girlie: "Freezing! I hate this time of the year."

Neighbor: "Did you have a nice Christmas?"

Girlie: "Yes, but now that it's all over, all that's left is this miserable weather. It gets darker and colder, and I can't do anything outdoors."

And here the conversation abruptly departed from the conventional rules of the perfect stranger interaction in England.

Neighbor: "Come on, it's not that bad! You shouldn't complain so much about the weather. And not at your age! You can still do some outdoor activities in the winter."

Girlie resisted the impulse to reply to the comment about her age and chose to politely return to the weather.

"Like what? I don't really like running or cycling in this weather. It's depressing."

Neighbor: "I think you should try polo. I'm not sure if you know how to ride a horse, or if you ever played golf before, but polo is like a combination of both. You can do it in the winter too, in an arena. We play at a club out in Windsor. There's an academy there too. Maybe you should give them a call."

Polo was not something the girl had ever thought about. She eyed him suspiciously as he carried on talking, telling her how much fun it was and that she should give it a try.

And then suddenly he turned around, whistled at his dog, said good-bye, and vanished into the fog. Girlie didn't know it then, but Ziggy's dad was like this. Unpredictable, straight to the point, and with no time for polite conversation.

Girlie took Bentley home and told her husband about the strange encounter.

He didn't think it would lead anywhere. But the following weekend, she checked out the club online and, without thinking about it too much, she booked an introductory polo lesson.

It was freezing cold when Girlie had her first lesson in the rain. Her husband came with her because he was a perfect gentleman, just as Girlie was the perfect lady, and he didn't want to leave her alone during this unpredictable adventure. He waited patiently for her, tucked away in the car with the heating on, thinking this would be the one and only time he would have to come here. Outside, a strong wind was blowing the soft winter rain in all directions. He could not see her, obscured by the tall walls of the arena, and wondered whether she would cut her lesson short and admit this was just a crazy idea. But when she came back to the car, she said with a wide grin, "I love it! I booked another lesson for next weekend!"

And so, with one short sentence, Girlie made a clear break with her former self. She was no longer predictable.

The following day she went to work, and this was when I noticed she could barely walk. We had a meeting to talk about one of the projects I was managing and for which her team needed to provide input. I waited patiently in the meeting room I had booked, wondering why she was late. Girlie was never late for meetings.

But then when she finally stepped through the door, it became apparent that she was limping. Her high heels made her steps even more difficult.

She sat gingerly in the chair in front of me and answered my unspoken question. "Sorry I'm late. I have a little problem walking today."

"What happened?" I asked, now concerned as to whether she was in any condition to even have this meeting.

"Oh, it's nothing." She shook her head. "It's just muscle pain. I had a riding lesson yesterday."

In a fraction of a second, the image of my riding boots started dancing in front of my eyes. Uninvited.

"Riding?" I was not sure why but I could barely breathe.

"Actually, I had a polo lesson. You know, polo on horseback? We didn't do much polo though, only riding, but I haven't been on a horse for a long time, and apparently this is what happens…" She waved her hand towards her legs. "Muscle pain."

I was still silent, wondering what it was that hit me so strongly and when it was going to go away and let me carry on with this meeting.

"But I'm here now, and I can talk, even if I can't walk properly." She smiled. "Let me log on to my computer, and we'll talk about this schedule you emailed me and the presentation next week. Just to make sure you've got all you need from my team."

I watched her in silence. I still couldn't talk. I could think of one word only: riding. I had made no effort to find an occasion to ride in these past two months. But it looked like riding had found me.

"Are you going again?" I asked.

She looked up from her computer screen, confused.

"Riding, I mean," I added. "Because if you are, I'd love to join you."

She nodded. I smiled. We had a deal and it seemed much more important than next week's presentation.

And so it happened that my riding boots got used after all. The following weekend, Girlie and I went to the polo club together.

It was still raining and pretty cold. We rode in the arena, in the rain. We each had a horse and an instructor. Hers was a patient middle-aged guy who smiled all the time. Mine looked like Richard Gere and was very serious. I wondered why I only got serious guys, but he was good-looking, so I didn't mind. Maybe he was going to be the *someone* I was looking for, I thought as I got into the saddle.

But then I couldn't think about anything any longer. I had no time. Long-buried memories of moving along with the horse's steps took over, and my body slowly regained its confidence in the saddle, as if those twenty-odd years since I'd last ridden had not passed, and I were a girl of eighteen again. They say riding a horse is like riding a bicycle. Your muscles will remember it for life.

I trotted, and I even cantered. I got to hold a polo mallet but did nothing with it. I realized that polo horses are led with one hand only, like cowboys' horses in the Western movies, and I thought this was awesome. I tried to chat with my instructor, but he wasn't very talkative. All he was interested in was giving orders.

"Heels lower. Back straight. Look up. Lead the horse to the right, now left. Now turn."

It was easier than I'd expected.

Then I jumped off the saddle into mud that came up to my ankles. But I was wearing my old riding boots, so I didn't mind. I also didn't mind the cold and the rain because I didn't have time to think about them. I wasn't thinking much about anything. I even didn't think too much when I told my instructor that I'd love to do it again. The following weekend.

When I saw Girlie at the car we'd both hired to get to the club, I told her with a wide grin that I'd booked another lesson.

"I booked one too," she said.

There was no explanation either of us could find for this sudden interest, so we didn't look for one. We just drove home with the heating in the car turned to the max, trying to warm up our aching muscles and chatting about how exciting our little riding experience had been.

A passion was born silently, and it happened in that arena, in the middle of the mud and in the rain. We both got hooked on polo.

The Thirteen Rules of Polo Wisdom

After my first lesson comes the second one. Then another one and another. Soon I have a regular appointment every Saturday morning with my coach who looks like Richard Gere, and the rain, the mud, and a different horse every time.

I bought the first polo helmet I could find at the farm shop next door. It happened to be a child-sized, black, simple three-point harness helmet. I promised myself I'd buy a really fancy, colorful polo helmet once I became a real player. For now, this one seemed suited to the job. I learned how to polish my boots after every lesson because my instructor said a polo player never comes on the field with unpolished boots. Mine weren't actually the fancy brown polo boots with a long zipper running across the front that I saw other riders wearing. They were just my old black riding boots, but I thought I should make an effort nevertheless. I was on my way to becoming a polo player, after all. So I showed up weekend after weekend for my polo lessons with my new helmet, my old boots, and every thick sweater I could find, piled on under a waterproof jacket.

And dating? Well, I still hadn't met anyone. But going to my polo lesson gave a purpose to my weekend, and I worried less about going out. That took the pressure off me to find someone immediately. I had something to do, something that left me smiling and happy, and then I needed a few days to recover from riding. My muscles still hurt, although my riding was getting better, and when one has muscles that hurt, one doesn't think about dating. Then I told myself I might meet someone at the club. After all, most dating websites recommended finding a mate you could share passions with. And now that I was discovering my passions, I thought maybe my love coach was right, and this could actually lead me to the man of my life. I just had to be patient and learn to play this game. Polo, I mean.

I usually drove to the polo club in a rented car. It was about an hour away from London, in Berkshire, the county that is known as Polo Land in England because it has more polo clubs than any other. I had lived more than ten years in London and never felt the need to buy a car. Girlie and I usually rode down together. After working together for about two years and barely exchanging a word outside the office, we had become instant best friends. Polo drove us both out of our cozy homes and into the frozen arena weekend after weekend.

I used to change into my riding gear in a tiny toilet usually used by the grooms. Ours was a very fancy polo club, one of the top in the country, but we weren't members. We soon learned that becoming a member of that club was quite different from just taking polo lessons there, but for now, as non-members, we had no access to the fancy clubhouse or the lockers.

After changing into my riding gear, I walked towards the arena, usually in mud up to my ankles, and jumped on a horse, usually onto a wet saddle. It rained most of the time. Sometimes it only drizzled, but that was worse than the rain since it was usually colder. Other times it poured down, but the school never canceled the lesson, and I couldn't bring myself to do so either. So I rode in the rain next to my coach, whom I decided to call Richard, after his lookalike. Richard told me that only clients could cancel lessons, and, as long as I didn't, he had to show up and do his job. I wondered sometimes if he secretly wished I would cancel, but I couldn't bring myself to do it, not even when it was pouring down so heavily that the horses walked sideways to avoid the drops hitting their eyes.

Saturday after Saturday I showed up and did exactly the same thing: rode a horse, obeyed instructions, and paid attention to every detail of my posture. If I wanted to be a polo player, I would first have to become a decent rider, Richard said.

On my second lesson, I had my first fall. I came off at a slow canter during my first attempt to hit the ball. Fortunately, the mud underneath was thick enough that it didn't hurt.

On my third lesson it rained so hard that the horse turned sideways in a desperate attempt to put its bum between its eyes and the rain. I got soaked to my underwear. Ever since, I've brought a full change of clothes whenever I play polo. Even in the middle of summer.

By my fourth lesson, I was well prepared for the rain. This time it was only a drizzle, but the wind was blowing, and it was so cold that all my muscles contracted. I shivered with cold all the way home, and dove immediately into a hot bath. That was the wrong thing to do, I found out soon afterwards, when a sharp back pain told me that having a hot bath was not the wisest thing to do after riding in the cold weather.

On my fifth lesson, nothing happened. That's because I had to cancel it. I was at home, in agony with back pain. That's when I met Morgan, my chiropractor. He got me back on my feet, and

I booked a regular appointment with him every Monday evening. This proved to be my wisest polo decision. Ever.

On my sixth lesson, the sun came out. By then I felt like a veteran. I started hoping that polo could somehow, miraculously, be more than rain, mud, cold, and the omnipresent instruction to "keep your knees in and your heels down!"

And on my seventh polo lesson something astonishing happened. I learned I could fly. I rose up from the saddle into the half-seat position polo players usually adopt during the game. They call it half seat because you're neither seated nor standing, but suspended somewhere in-between, your trousers barely touching the saddle, your body weight supported by your knees deeply pushed into the saddle, the balls of your feet pressing strongly into the stirrups. I could hold the position for a few minutes only before collapsing back into the saddle, but my coach had a big smile on his face, and at the end of that lesson, he told me that we could now start to hit the ball.

Then, for a few lessons, we did exactly that; we hit balls. Well, I *tried* to hit them and found out there were a thousand ways one could miss a ball. But Richard didn't care. "Just try again," he said every time I missed.

And at some point—I'm not sure which lesson it was, since I had lost count of them—spring broke out. All of a sudden, it was sunny and not that cold any longer. And I could finally ride. Even by the tough standards of my coach, I could ride. My stops were subtle enough, my heels low enough, my posture almost elegant enough for his taste. And the pain in my back reached bearable levels for the first time in three months.

And that was when I went out and bought my first pair of white polo jeans.

About the same time, I realized that polo was not just polo. It was a new philosophy of life. So I started writing down The Rules, as shouted across the field by my tireless coach.

1. On first things first:
Coach on lesson one: "Breathe…" Lesson two: "Breathe…" Lesson three: "Breathe…"

Me: "When do we talk about riding?"

Coach: "You can't ride if you don't breathe. First of all you need to learn to relax."

2. On the right level of detail:
Coach, repetitive to the level of obsession: "Look at the ball! Look at the ball! Look at the ball!"

Me, frustrated: "I'm looookiiiing!!"

Coach, calm: "Not enough. When you really look at the ball, you will start seeing the grass between the ball and the earth!"

3. On recognizing what's yours:
Canter towards the ball. Lean towards the ball. Ball too far away, so I lean a bit more. Fall from the horse on top of the ball. Horse stops with that "another one bites the dust" expression in his eyes.

Me: silent, busy clearing the dust out of my mouth.

Coach, patiently: "This ball wasn't yours, wasn't meant for you. Why did you try so hard to get it? If it's not perfect, don't even try to hit it—you'll only hurt yourself."

Results: two weeks of back pain.

4. On teamwork:
"Follow your teammate. If he misses the ball, you hit it. If you miss it, your teammate who is following you will get it."

5. On thinking:
First shot: miss. Second shot: miss. Third shot: miss.

Me, frustrated: "Why is it not happening?"

Coach, chilled: "Because you're too keen. Stop thinking about it, and it will happen."

6. On control:
Coach, annoyed: "What are you doing with that wrist of yours, getting in the way of the stick? The stick knows its job. It's got weight, and gravity pulls it. What do you think you are going to achieve, trying to control where the stick goes? You're only going to hurt your wrist! Get out of the way and let the stick do its job!"

7. On sacrifices:
Coach: "Heels down. Heels down. Heels down."

Me: "I can't keep my heels lower than this—they're used to high heels!"

Coach: "Stop wearing high heels if you want to stay in the saddle."

8. On trust:
Coach: "Stop looking back! When you drop the mallet, have confidence that the stick will find the ball. You don't need to look!"

9. On positive thinking:
I ride towards the ball, hit, and miss.

Coach, relaxed: "Stop thinking about it. Erase this from your mind immediately. Now. Ride on, don't stop. Ride on and enjoy the ride."

10. On perspective:
Coach: "Stop looking at the horse. He's still there, and he will do what you want him to do. Keep your head up and your eyes looking across the field. That's where you're playing, not at the horse's level."

11. On horses and boyfriends:
Coach: "Be firm but respectful with the horse. Ride with a purpose. Be clear about what you want from him, and he will listen. Otherwise he'll start thinking he can lead this game. Remember, horses are like boyfriends. Be firm and they will listen."

12. On the bigger picture:

Coach: "It's not about the ball. Stop chasing the ball. Just do your job, enjoy the ride, and the ball will come to you!"

13. On effortless perfection:

Coach, enthusiastically: "Wow, that was a perfect shot! How did it feel?"

Me, uncertainly: "I don't know. I didn't feel much. Somehow easy, like there was no effort, but I didn't have time to think about it…"

Coach, smiling: "Exactly. Now you know how the perfect shot feels. Effortless!"

Once a Knight, Always a Knight

SUMMER

Summer comes, and I still have no boyfriend. But I have a car, a cute little blue-and-white Mini. I buy it because I'm tired of renting a car to get to the polo field. It's my first significant polo purchase. And I have something else, a new identity: I have become a polo player.

It doesn't happen technically until June, because I can't be a polo player before I actually play my first game, but then one day this threshold is crossed as well.

"You're ready," my coach said one Saturday morning as I turned up for my regular practice. I expected it would be just like the other training sessions: ride, hit balls, miss balls, and get a refresher on all the dos and don'ts. For my coach, polo had always been a very precise game.

Richard was like this, very detail-oriented and precise. "Heels, one inch lower," he used to say. "Elbows back, not so much. Lean forward. Too much, less so…" And then the long-awaited validation: "Yes, that's right, perfect!"

I had become addicted to perfection, just for him. He was a nice guy, my coach, and for a few lessons I thought that maybe something would happen between us, but he was a true professional who did not use polo as his flirting ground. And there was another reason, a reason I was to find out much later. My coach, like other polo coaches, was a little tired of all the single women who took up polo in the hope they would *meet someone*. But for now, my polo connections were limited to my coach—always the same—and Girlie.

"Ready for what?" I asked him.

"Today we play," he said. "Just a chukka, don't worry," he added, probably seeing the shock on my face. "A practice game. We'll go slow. You and me on one side, Girlie and her instructor on the other side. You're both ready!"

Ready? I felt anything but. But life is like that, sometimes. There comes a time, after months of practice, when all you can do is throw all those carefully rehearsed movements out the window, and all that's left is the wind on your face, the smell of the horse in your nostrils, and the adrenaline in your blood. And ready or not, you go out there and give it your best, because there's a time to learn, and there's a time to play. And the horse, the mallet, and the ball, they all melt and become one with you, and you melt too and become one with the field and the wind…

And that's all I remembered from my first chukka. We must have gone ridiculously slowly. I probably missed three balls for each one I hit. But it didn't matter. All I knew is that we were playing at last, and this made all the difference. And from that moment onwards, five months after our initial lessons, we had officially become polo players.

And dating? Well, dating almost disappeared from my radar in the months after this first chukka. I had no time for dating, no time to go out, because I was spending all my weekends at the club. And no interest either, I discovered to my astonishment. I had enough excitement in my life and didn't desperately feel the need for a boyfriend any longer. It would have been nice to have someone of course, but… what if he were not into polo? This would have been a disaster. So I decided to add a new "must have" to the list of boxes *someone* needed to tick: play polo.

And where best to find a boyfriend who played polo than in a polo club?

Towards the middle of the summer, I finally started socializing at the club. After our first practice game together, Girlie and I were allowed to join other beginners in what they called "chill-out chukkas"—very easy games. These were slow games with no scoring and a coach playing on each team. There was no umpire, only the coaches shouting instructions across the field. But this was enough to make us feel like proper polo players, and after our little instructional game, we carried our dirty white jeans with great pride into the clubhouse and mingled with the real players, sipping a glass of Pimm's or, more often in my case, a Campari orange. And we talked.

Girlie usually led the conversation. Things were easy for Girlie, as she didn't need to hunt for *someone*. She'd been happily married for more than fifteen years. How does someone stay happily married for fifteen years? I wondered. My longest relationship had been five years, with most of them anything but happy.

Many players had dogs and brought them over to the clubhouse for after-polo mingling. Girlie's Bentley, the perfect dog, was there, and so was Ziggy, so I finally got to meet his owner, the man who so unexpectedly got us into polo. And there were countless other dogs, sweet Dalmatians, tall greyhounds, a bored-looking German shepherd, a huge South African hunting dog—my favorite—and various other unidentified mixed breeds. We each had our role: Girlie talked to the owners as I petted the dogs. Maybe this was why she was married and I was single.

I called them "darling" and flirted with them. The dogs, I mean. Not the players, God forbid! I found out that overnight I had been rendered extremely shy, as if my old desire to meet someone had been washed away by my new desire to become a proper polo player. And how could I be a proper polo player if I flirted with other polo players? I needed to play with them, not flirt with them!

This had become a difficult business. I wanted my *someone* to play polo, but I soon learned that I was useless at flirting with my polo buddies. Not that anyone wanted to flirt with me anyway.

So I contented myself with sipping my Campari orange, petting the dogs, listening to Girlie chat, and thinking maybe I should take chatting lessons from her. And after a while I ended up dragging myself home because the post-game exhaustion kicked in very quickly after a drink. I didn't meet *someone*, but who cared? I was a polo player!

And I realized there was an added benefit to being a polo player. It sounded very appealing to non-polo players. Outside my circle of players at the club, in my everyday life, I found that women were envious and men intrigued. And everyone kept on asking me the same question over and over again:

"So, why is it that you play polo?"

Whatever I did, I could not escape the question. Only taking refuge at the polo club saved me from it, maybe because others were taking refuge from similar questions. But when I had to face the outside world, I developed two answers: the official one and the unofficial one.

The official one was along the lines of "It's amazing." I usually got blank stares back. I followed up with "There's nothing like it." Identical blank stares. Then, feeling the need to explain, I carried on, talking about becoming one with the horse, the adrenaline of the game, the quick decisions, too quick to think. The mind that stopped as never before. The team spirit. The danger. The sensation of flying on the back of the horse. Usually the blank stares started to melt at this point, giving way to polite nods. I wasn't sure, though, that people understood. It's very difficult for people who don't play polo to understand the real reason why people do play polo. They seem to have a lot of ideas in their head about why people play, and when they ask a question, they usually seek a confirmation of their beliefs:

"Is it because all the princes play polo? Have you met any princes yet?"

"Is it because of the parties? I hear the polo parties are great!"

"Is it because it's such an exclusive game?"

"Is it because of the men? The polo players? Are they really so amazing?"

Non-polo players were convinced they knew why polo players played polo. And when their questions didn't get the answers they expected, they smiled politely and nodded with a look on their face that said, *I know, I know… You just don't want to admit it!*

I usually talked about the communion with the horse and about how *it feels like flying*, while the initiator of the conversation went back to questions about the parties, the polo players, and the princes. We stopped talking after a few polite exchanges. They kept their opinion. I saved my speech for the next time.

The unofficial answer was the one I reserved for close friends and those well tested in their tolerance for my weirdness. My unofficial answer went like this:

"I play polo because I think I'm a reincarnated knight."

I kept a straight face when I delivered this message, but I usually did so as we were having a drink. It was a good trick, mixing this answer with a drink. Those who believed me did so in spite of it, and those who didn't blamed it on the drink. And I got to tell the truth.

But whether they believed me or not, I remembered exactly

how it felt. The horse between your knees, alive, full of adrenaline, ready to go. The horse leaping forward at the slightest squeeze of your knees. The left hand locked down on the reins, although it's with your body and not with the reins that you direct the horse. And sometimes you drive him with your look, as if you have melted into the animal and you are he, and he is you, and together you've a single purpose: survival. Your right hand holds a long and heavy object that you hit with. You hit as if your life depends on it. You look after your people, and you try to fight *the others*. Sometimes it's tough, sometimes you lose. Other times you win. But the adrenaline is always there and that old feeling of going into battle. I was convinced this is how they felt centuries ago when they put on their armor, mounted their horse, held the sword in their right hand, the horse's reins in the left, said a short prayer, and went into battle.

And maybe football is so popular because footballers are the reincarnated infantry of all the wars of the world. Far more numerous than the knights. The same feeling without horses. Maybe. I don't know for sure. I'm not a reincarnated infantry soldier, and I never was a football fan.

I once was a knight.

And so were those I play with.

As I line up for the start of the chukka, and we fall silent in those last seconds before the ball is thrown in, the guy to my right leans over and whispers to me:

"Do you think this is how they felt? Back then, I mean, when they lined up ready for battle?"

I'm speechless. I've never told him my unofficial answer. But maybe he feels it too. And there's no time to say anything anyway. The umpire has thrown the ball in and the old cry for battle fills my ears:

"Plaaaay!"

Polo Fever

SEPTEMBER

Autumn comes and brings the sudden realization that the polo season is about to end. Soon there will be no more chill-out chukkas on our small polo school field, nothing like the full-size polo fields but more of a cabbage patch, slightly on a slope and with a few divots that the horses regularly trip on. But for me, it's heaven. And I'm about to lose my heaven.

There was, of course, a winter alternative: polo in the arena. But after one tastes the wide-open green fields, one does not look forward to being locked up in a muddy arena again. Besides, I was no longer a beginner, and the arena reminded me of my first polo lessons. Now, I was a polo player. Or so I thought.

All I could think about was how I could play more polo. Where I could play more polo. It was then I heard that Argentina was the best country for polo, and all serious professional polo players moved to Argentina as soon as the polo season ended in England.

Argentina is well below the equator, and this has the advantage of reversing the seasons: when winter kicks in here, summer starts over there. Perfect, I thought. I had to go to Argentina. One day. I wanted to be a polo player, so I 'd better do what polo players did.

Towards the end of the season, I watched my coach take a nasty fall and break a couple of ribs. His horse tripped, and he flew out of the saddle. Although he was visibly in pain, he got back on the horse and managed to finish the lesson. Afterwards, I had lessons from another coach for a few weeks because Richard was unable to get back into the saddle. I thought nothing of it all—just a really bad-luck day. After all, Richard was one of the most exquisite riders I had ever met. A rider like that doesn't come out of the saddle easily. It must have been bad luck. No thought crossed my mind that this type of bad luck could happen to me one day. I was still living with fever. Polo fever.

And something else was making me uneasy. Autumn meant my birthday was approaching, and with it the one-year anniversary of my fateful encounter with the love coach. A small bubble of irritation started to boil away inside: I had followed her advice, reconnected with a long-forgotten passion—riding, and discovered a new one—polo. I'd spent about nine months looking after myself and indulging in my newfound passion. That's about the same time it takes a woman to make a baby. But this didn't get me any closer to meeting someone. Here I was, about to turn thirty-nine and still single!

With the polo season ending, I started to panic again and turned my interest towards going out with non-polo people. My summer at the club, with all its mingling and dog petting, yielded no boyfriend.

So I went on a blind date arranged by a friend. I met a handsome, successful, late-thirties entrepreneur. Just like all the other non-polo people, he was impressed that I played polo. I felt good. I didn't know it then, but it turned out being impressed with a girl and being attracted to her were two totally different things in a man's mind.

"How about the rest of your life?" he asked me after about an hour of polo-related conversation.

Hmm… there wasn't much to say. Go to work, come home, go to the polo club. My once-a-week routine had evolved into three or four times a week over the summer.

"Not much else to say," I admitted eventually. "I love polo so much that I got into the habit of dating horses!" I added, pleased I managed to find a joke to explain my single status.

A quick glance at him was enough to realize he didn't take it as a joke. The horror in his eyes said it all. Our conversation died pretty quickly afterwards. We said good-bye, and I never saw him again.

Too bad, I thought. He seemed a nice guy. But he obviously wasn't into polo. And he had no sense of humor either.

So I went alone to the big end-of-the-polo-season party organized by my club. Everyone was there with their partners; Girlie was with her husband, and the many guys I'd met during the summer in the clubhouse while patting their dogs were there with their wives and girlfriends as well. I guess men playing polo are far more attractive to women than the other way around. There were very few single people there. One of them was Richard, my coach.

"How are your ribs?" I asked him. "Are you ready to get back on the horse?"

He smiled. Of course he was ready. There's no question about a polo player being ready to get back on a horse.

"The ribs are the worst," he said. "You can't protect them. We play in T-shirts, so there's nothing we can do. But all the rest, remember my words, Roxy, use as much protection as you can: ankle pads, elbow pads. And a face guard. It's about time you started playing with a face guard. Because when things happen—and I don't say *if*—*when* things happen, you'll be glad you had all the protection you could get."

I nodded, smiled and raised my glass of champagne. The chairman of our club was about to make his annual address, and silence set in. Besides, who wanted to talk about injuries at a polo party anyway?

It was good to have him back, I thought. And interesting that he came alone. I wondered why there was no woman in his life. I watched him out of the corner of my eyes as the chairman went on and on: tall forehead, strong jaw, black hair with a hint of gray. He must have been in his late forties but he looked very fit. Of course he was fit: he was a polo player. A polo player. A single polo player.

Maybe going back in the arena for the winter season wouldn't be so bad after all…

One-Way Ticket to Argentina

NOVEMBER

Click click click. It's done. I've bought it. My one-way ticket to Argentina.

I pause for a few seconds to think about what I've just done. There is an uncomfortable feeling somewhere at the base of my throat, but I push it down. It will be okay, I tell myself. After all, my huge polo gear bag bears a big logo: "Follow your passion." So I decide to follow mine, all the way to Argentina.

"Be careful with polo." I hear in my mind the calm voice of my polo coach. "It's very addictive. I know people who tried it and got so hooked that they started losing everything: their money, their house, their job, their friends. Polo can drive people nuts. Be careful how you manage it."

No, no, this isn't addiction. This is passion. I love this sport. But the uncomfortable feeling at the base of my throat tells me there's a very fine line between the two, and I'm walking right down the middle of it.

The polo pull was strong. I'd been learning and playing for over ten months now. It had slowly taken over most of my free time: my social life, my weekends, my dinner conversations. Now I was giving it a month, maybe more. I wasn't sure when I'd come back.

All of a sudden my life had opened up. The project I'd been working on for the past two years for a large multinational came to an end. There was no other work in sight, and I didn't feel much like looking for any. Working as a freelancer had its ups and downs. In my job, the downs were pretty clear: being treated like a mercenary by the companies who hired you, no security, job offers coming and going, projects that looked certain one day and went up in smoke the next. There was one up: freedom. The ability to take time off and do whatever you wanted. In my case, to follow my passion.

So I decided to go. The summer polo season had ended in England, the sky was dark, and I couldn't cope with being trapped in the muddy arena again. This was not the polo I had come to love. Not after tasting the big open spaces, not after playing in sunshine. Not after the summer. I couldn't go back into the arena. Richard, my coach, reverted back to his polite self every time I had a lesson, and my fantasies slowly faded away. No, he wasn't meant to be my *someone*, my polo player. I had to look harder—and elsewhere.

Argentina seemed the perfect answer to all my issues. It would take me back to the sun, so I could avoid the gray skies in England. It would also take me back to open field polo so I could forget about the muddy arena. And it was filled with handsome polo players—or so I imagined—and who knew what might happen in a faraway land filled with handsome polo players? *I need a holiday*, I told myself. *And I need to meet someone.*

I shrug and turn off my computer. It's done now, so there's no point having second thoughts. I've never been to Argentina, haven't booked any hotel accommodation, and know no one there. But it isn't the first time I've jumped into the unknown. Things have a funny way of working out in the end. I'd found that out many years ago, in Africa, in the middle of another adventure that just worked out. It was there that a guide in the desert told me something powerful that I have never forgotten: "The world belongs to those who dream."

And these days, I dreamed of a green polo field, shining in the bright sun, filled with handsome polo players. And one of them would be mine.

One week later, when I land for the first time in Argentina, I find out that at least one of my dreams has been fulfilled: the morning sun is shining stronger than anything I remember in England.

Maybe it's simply because in Argentina, November is the equivalent of May, and spring has just settled in. Or maybe it's because we've landed early in the morning, and after a night spent awake in the darkness, crammed into a tiny economy-class seat, anything would feel like arriving in paradise.

I find my two suitcases and the huge polo bag, and proceed to the exit to look for a man with my name on a piece of paper. That's because when you jump into the unknown, the Universe rallies to your side and sends you a guardian angel. Mine was called Marco. He must have been a saint in a previous life. Or maybe I had been the saint, and he owed me. I wasn't sure why, but every time I needed help he was there, my soul brother, former schoolmate, and friend for life. He was always there when I needed a shoulder to cry on or advice about love or the lack of it in my life. He was usually there on the other side of a phone line, because he lived in Italy and traveled for work all over the world, and I lived in England and spent my spare time on polo fields. All this meant it was difficult to meet face to face. Nevertheless, he was there, and he'd been there for the past thirteen years since we'd met and become friends in the corridors of the business school in Italy where we both studied for our MBAs.

As soon as I booked my one-way flight, I needed a shoulder to cry on, because I had second thoughts, no matter how hard I pushed them away. And Marco was my shoulder of choice. So I called him. It turned out he was not only a saint in his ability to listen to my problems, but he had the supernatural ability to create perfect scenarios as well.

"I'll send someone to pick you up from the airport when you arrive. And we'll dine together," he said in his usual matter-of-fact voice.

"In Buenos Aires? Marco, it's Argentina, not Italy!"

"Precisely, *amore*."

Marco either called me *amore*, which means love, or *imbecille*, idiot, depending on the mood he was in and the type of story I was telling him.

He was in a good mood today, I deduced.

"I'll be there on a business trip. I go there quite often these days, and I can easily arrange to be there when you land. I'll send a taxi driver to pick you up. He's a good guy, Luciano, he usually drives me around when I'm there, and I know him well."

Yes, he's definitely a saint.

Soon I'm comfortably seated across the table from this saint in a small Italian restaurant in the middle of the Palermo district of Buenos Aires. I checked into the hotel he recommended, trusted his driver to take me there, and didn't even ask where we were going when I met my friend in the lobby.

"So, *imbecille*… here you are. I didn't believe you'd go ahead with this crazy idea, but, hey, you still manage to surprise me sometimes."

Marco eats his pizza with delicate and precise movements, cutting each slice with a knife and fork but then eating with his fingers. The way all Italians do. I watch him as he chews a mouthful, and I smile. He's just as I remember him. Elegant, crisp white shirt, a black cardigan casually thrown across his shoulders and loosely knotted around his neck. The understated elegance of Northern Italy. A short beard that earned him the nickname of *cane lupo*—wolfhound—and a carefully guarded neutral expression on his face. Marco loved delivering his sarcastic comments with a poker face.

"It's not so crazy. I'm here to play polo," I tell him. "And I'm not at all an *imbecille*. I know exactly what I want."

"And that is?" He smiles and stops chewing for a few seconds.

"I want to play polo. I want to get away from winter in England. And I want to meet someone."

"You want to meet someone? Here?" He looks at me, half amused, half serious. "And what's wrong with London?"

"I haven't met anyone in London for a long while," I admit.

"How long?"

"Longer than I want to think about," I say, avoiding the uncomfortable truth.

"I think your last heartbreak was… hmm, let's see… When was the last time you called me for an intensive coaching session? Last year? No, I don't think so. It must have been two years ago, in summer, right?"

Marco has always been very good with figures.

"Right." I shrug. "No one since."

"At least you didn't get your heart broken again, either. *Imbecille*."

Marco has a funny way of seeing the good in everything.

"Yeah. That's the benefit. But look, I'm fed up. I'm ready to meet someone. I even hired a love coach who told me to get in touch with my passions. And I did, I mean, look, I'm playing polo. I found a new passion. Now I'm ready to find him. My man, I mean."

"Roxy, listen."

I look at him, expecting an *imbecille,* but, no, Marco is a man of sudden changes.

"*Amore,* take care. This country is fun, but men are not serious here. Really, they're not. Take it easy, enjoy your holiday. Play polo if you must. Then go back home, find another project, and look for someone there, in England. In your world. Not here."

"What's wrong with *here*? And I'm not necessarily looking for an Argentine. I'm looking for a polo player."

"And how do you plan to go about that?" he asks with a voice close to boredom.

"I'm going to start with the polo *estancias.* That's polo clubs that offer lodging and instructions. I'm going to go around and play at a few of them and see who I meet. And improve my game too."

And to this he has no answer. No *amore* and no *imbecille* either.

After all, I'm just a girl looking for love in a faraway country. And if there isn't any love to be found, playing polo isn't such a bad second option.

Dale Monica

DECEMBER

"*Dale*, Monica! *Dale, Dale, vamos!*" I tell him I'm Roxy, but Monica seems to please him more, so I settle on being Monica for now. He rides behind me, and I get my horse into a canter again. The ball is in front of me: head over the ball, lean out, swing, hit. Again… again… again…

My back is arched, my body is crying out, every little bone in my back is sore, but he rides behind me and passes over every single ball I miss, and I have to carry on. Strangely enough, I don't miss that many balls these days; it's as if my polo has got better overnight simply because I've landed in the country of polo—Argentina.

I ride in the morning until I'm close to exhaustion and my horse simply refuses to go for another run. I ride until I feel he's about to buck me off, and then, grateful that it's over, I turn and walk him slowly to the stables, wondering if my knees will give in once I jump off. I ride in the afternoons with them, the Argentine polo players, who ride like they were born on horses. They ride with no hard hats, no knee or elbow pads. They ride in jeans and T-shirts with their hair flowing freely in the wind, and I smile and realize how ridiculous we look with all our protective equipment and hard hats. I ride alongside them, wishing my hair were free in the wind…

"*Dale*, Monica! Put your boobs out and your bum out as well, like this." He arches his back in the perfect pose of a polo player in full swing—or a pole dancer, same thing really. "You see, like this, boobs out!" I smile at his directness. This would have been a bit too explicit for an English coach, but here it seems perfectly acceptable. I try to imagine myself pole dancing. I swing and hit, a plain, clean hit, and the ball goes halfway across the field. "You see?" He smiles. "Boobs out and the ball goes far!" I now think of pole dancing every time I hit, but it's a really difficult thing: my arched back makes my muscles hurt even more. "I know, I know." His smile is kind. "I know, more difficult, but better hit." And I get it suddenly: the pain is there, but the trick is to allow it to be there, and arch your back despite the pain, and hit, again… again… again…

I play with them again in the afternoon. I play as number one (weakest position), and I'm told to mark the number four (strongest position) from the opposite team, and I can't even get close to him. The only time I try to hook him, I miss, and I'm grateful that I missed, since his swing is so powerful I would most probably have been thrown out of the saddle. I ride close to him, and then I feel he's about to ride me off, and this would be the end of me and my horse as well, but he knows better. He comes close and shouts "Taco, taco!" just to frighten me, and then, in full gallop, he grabs the ears of my horse and laughs, galloping away. He doesn't need to ride me off; I get the message totally and fully. It's his ball, and I graciously move out of his way.

I ride with them every day, and every time I get off my horse, my body aches and refuses to think about ever getting back on a horse. I crawl into bed for the noon siesta, and I promise myself that I'll not get on a horse again that day. But the afternoon comes, and we're due to play. It's a four-chukka game, and by chukka two,

I almost cry out in pain. I'm out of breath, and I feel like bailing out, but then I remember I'll miss the handshakes at the end if I do, and this thought keeps me going. And I move on, with him riding behind me shouting "*Dale*, Monica!", with the smiley guy I'm supposed to mark far in the distance. I ride in the late afternoon sun with the smell of freshly cut grass in my nostrils. I ride despite the pain in my body and despite the weakness in my knees. I ride, and I don't think of anything but the ball, the horse, the fact that the game appears to be turning, and I need to change direction. I ride, not knowing sometimes which way we are supposed to go and whether that was a real goal or not, but I ride on. I ride with them, and their joy of riding spreads to me, and for a few moments I feel there's nothing else to life but riding…

By the third chukka, I'm given a very narrow horse with a shiny leather saddle. My legs are almost giving in by this time, and I cringe when I think I'll probably end up on the horse's neck. I'm too tired to keep myself stable on a shiny leather saddle. But he's there and reads my thoughts: He asks me if I want some water. Water? No. Another horse maybe. But he smiles, takes a bottle of water, pours it all over my saddle, and tells me to rub my trousers against it. Now I look like I've been peeing in my trousers, or even worse, because the brown color of the saddle comes out on my white jeans. But it's okay actually, because now the wet leather grips like never before, and I smile, really grateful for this trick, and I know I'll be safe for another chukka. "*Dale*, Monica." The chukka has started without a whistle, without a lineup, and without notice, flowing on as naturally as everything these people do on their horses. I run out, mad, in full gallop across the field. I run flat out, and smile when I feel the solid grip of my wet leather saddle, and I know I'll now be able to stay safely on this horse.

Tomorrow I'll be back in Buenos Aires. I'll be sipping champagne, watching the finals of the Open, and spending my evenings in trendy restaurants and clubs with elegant people and wearing my high heels (if my legs don't give out), but today I'm still wearing my dusty boots *en el campo*—in the fields—with them, playing the game they so naturally master. Today I'm still one of them, and today I can still think of nothing. With a blank empty brain I ride and ride and ride… *Dale*, Monica!

Por Amor al Polo

JANUARY

My head is still sore from last night's New Year's Eve party, which took place in the middle of the Argentine campo. It was a great party. I took enough painkillers to numb my aching legs, and I danced until I could no longer move. By that time it was almost morning, and I collapsed into a deep, dreamless sleep for a few hours. And now, the flight. And no number of painkillers can deal with my sore head and even sorer back.

I am flying back to London because there's no way I'm able to sit on a horse any longer. I've overdone it, and nothing I try to do to fix my back helps: chiropractors, acupuncture, massage, spinal elongations, painkillers. Lots of painkillers. I even try self-hypnosis. No results. My body has completely and totally broken down. In some mysterious way, my back muscles have decided that there's no way they can cope any longer with the same amount of polo they used to do in a month, concentrated into a day. No way.

So only four weeks after my Argentinean adventure started, I have to bring it to an abrupt stop. Was it really worth it?

I close my eyes. The annoying buzz of the airplane is there. I try to push it away and return to Argentina in my mind, to be once again riding in the fields, the wheat touching my boots. Riding with the grooms in the early morning. Riding among the cattle, all seven hundred that belonged to the family who so kindly invited me to spend Christmas and New Year with them.

I arrived in Argentina knowing no one. I am leaving now feeling that I have a family there and friends I've known for a lifetime.

⌘

After I spent the first couple of weeks playing polo in two different polo estancias, I came back to Buenos Aires and decided to have a rest in the city. I met a friend of a friend, who told me I absolutely had to go to one more polo estancia. A polo farm some two hours away from Buenos Aires. It wasn't a commercial estancia like the other places and didn't cater to large groups. It was a family business. Her friend Gabriela and her partner, professional polo player Patricio, were welcoming paying polo guests into their home for intensive training sessions. So, I would stay with them and play some polo.

I wasn't tempted at first because I wouldn't meet any other players there, and my mind was still set on finding my polo player. But she insisted and told me I had to go, for a couple of days at least, to experience this authentic place in the Argentine pampas. So I booked it for three days and I went, never suspecting that this decision would change my life forever.

I met Patricio first when I arrived at the farm. A well-built polo player in his late thirties, with a heap of dark blond hair running wild. Tall forehead, deep green eyes, and a serious-looking face. Polite and well mannered, he spoke impeccable English and gave me a kiss on both cheeks, unlike the usual Argentine greeting, which consists of a kiss on the right cheek only.

He took my bags to my room, the only guest room they had at

the farm, and told me the horses had been prepared for a stick-and-ball session.

I met Gabriela after riding. She played polo too, although not professionally. She was extrovert and friendly, half Swiss and half Mexican, and was now living in Argentina with her boyfriend and their four-year-old son.

The next morning they took me for a ride, and this was when it finally hit me.

"Do you realize how you live here? Do you sometimes stop and think about how blessed you are to be here, in the middle of these fields? To wake up to these views and hear the singing of the campo in the early morning?" I asked them, breathless after a gallop in the flat fields surrounding their farm, the sun in my eyes, and the countless birds of the pampas awake and singing to a new morning.

Gabriela and Patricio, still on their horses, looked at each other and smiled politely. They must have thought I was crazy. But I was not. I just happened to know how it felt to commute to work by the London Underground every day. I couldn't explain this to them. Not at seven o'clock in the morning sunshine while we rode bareback in the fields. Not as we went back to the farm for an exquisite breakfast. Not even later as we started to stick and ball in the field in front of their house. Actually, there was no moment during the day when I could explain what I really meant. London, with its morning rush, lack of sun for six months of the year, high-pressure jobs, and tiny flats, was a world that didn't exist any longer. It had simply melted away.

Argentina, on the other hand, felt like the world as it used to be, before it lost its senses. It was a paradox, because nothing worked in the country, apparently. So they said. The economy was on the rocks, and the government wasn't really trusted by anyone. There were high rates of inflation, uncertainty, poverty, and international bond defaults. But people were happy, hospitable, and real. People made friends easily: They welcomed you, a stranger, into their families and their lives. People gave you a kiss on the cheek as soon as they met you. Here, people had not forgotten how to be human.

Argentina still held on to how things used to be before health and safety and all sorts of other regulations strangled our lives. Here, four-year-old kids still rode horses without helmets, neighbors got together to play polo in blue jeans, not the posh white jeans that were mandatory at our clubs. Here, horses roamed free in the field. Dogs ran on the polo field, and they had become skilled at avoiding the balls. Farm owners rode out in the morning to check on their cattle, and friends dropped by casually for an *assado* (barbecue). In London, I needed to schedule a dinner four weeks in advance, on average.

I rode horses at their farms and marveled at the peace of the pampas until I could neither ride nor walk any longer. Then I took refuge again in a hotel in Buenos Aires and asked the receptionist to send a massage therapist to my room. She arrived promptly, nicely dressed in a uniform like that of a nurse. Actually, I needed a nurse more than I needed a massage therapist.

I opened the door and showed her in. I couldn't walk straight. Using the few Spanish words I knew, I told her about the back pain and playing polo. She smiled. She knew all about polo, she said. Everyone in this country knew about polo, one way or the other. She told me to lie down on the yoga mat I had brought with me all the way from London.

I screamed as soon as she touched me.

"Why did you do this to your body?" she asked in a sudden dramatic tone, probably tired of my cries.

"*Por amor al polo.* For the love of polo," I replied, mirroring the drama in her voice.

"*Hay amores que matan!* There are loves that kill!" she said, without smiling this time.

Yes, there are loves that may kill. But with a double dose of painkillers and a night of partying in the campo… well, it had been worth it.

I went back to the farm in the middle of the campo because Gabriela called and asked how I was. A courtesy call, I thought. I told her that I was all right and she shouldn't worry about me.

But she decided otherwise. She is one tough cookie, Gabriela. Once she sets her mind to something, there's no way around it. She invited me to spend Christmas at the farm.

I couldn't ride any longer, so I politely declined. But she made it clear it wasn't a riding invitation, that I wasn't being invited as a paying guest but rather as a friend. They were concerned about my spending Christmas alone and in pain at a Buenos Aires hotel.

So I went. I spent Christmas with them and their extended family. I had no idea how extended an extended family could be in Argentina, but I soon found out. We went to another farm belonging to a cousin of theirs, and met about fifty people. I had to kiss all of them as carefully instructed by Gabriela: one kiss only, on the right cheek. Then at midnight they started kissing again; I thought they were new arrivals and proceeded to introduce myself and kiss everyone who kissed me. Eventually, I realized I was kissing the same people I'd kissed when I arrived, who were now kissing to celebrate the start of Christmas Day. Then when I left, I had to kiss everyone again. I remember a lot of kissing that night, and it was all very new for me, a foreigner, the only foreigner in the family gathering in the middle of the *campo*.

The buzz of the plane is still there, filling my ears, taking me away from this world, second by second. Away from all the things I have come to love here. Away from polo, the reason why I came, but now a secondary concern. Away from all these smiley and welcoming people, from the farms, the horses, the open spaces. Away from the song of the campo in the early morning…

Yes, I came here *por amor al polo*. And now that I was

leaving, I realized that *mi corazon* had become, mysteriously and unexpectedly, *Argentino*.

Back to Where I Belong

FEBRUARY

"Ro, seriously, I'm coming back! Can I stay with you?"

On the other end of the phone, there's no hesitation in her voice despite the shock of this sudden announcement.

"Roxy, of course! But are you sure? Coming back so soon? Can you afford this?"

I'm not sure if I can afford it or not, but I'm trying not to think too much about it. I need to return to Argentina. The need originates somewhere at the level of my stomach and rises up to my heart. It's like a sort of heartburn. I have not yet digested this experience, and it calls me back.

It's only February. I came back to England last month and took some time out in order for my spine to recover. There was nothing broken, thankfully, just some very sore and tight muscles that refused to move. Gently, after countless sessions of massage and physiotherapy, the pain gradually went away. I knew I was supposed to focus on finding a new work project; after all, polo had already kept me out of work for nearly ten months. The consulting market was buoyant in February. It's like all recruiters wake up after the Christmas slumber and start spreading their nets again. And companies want to get going with new projects. I should have been putting my CV out there hoping to find one. But I couldn't do it. Something in me, something much stronger than my rational mind, was calling me back to Argentina, back to the pampas. Back to the inexplicable feeling of home I had unexpectedly encountered there. I had to go back.

This time it was not going to be expensive polo estancias and hotels in Buenos Aires, I decided. I had spent quite a lot of money in December, and I still had enough sense left to understand I couldn't do it all over again. Not fully, I mean. I would play some polo, I told myself, but this was going to be a different kind of a trip. A business trip. A new thought had nestled in my mind and refused to budge, no matter how hard I tried to extract it.

Maybe I could stay there forever. Find a way to live and work in Argentina.

I didn't speak Spanish, so looking for a consulting project there seemed out of the question. But maybe I could set up a business there. Something related to polo? A polo estancia? Maybe I could take people for polo training at the polo estancias I had been to and earn a handsome commission. Or even just play polo for free in exchange; that would be enough for me.

My business mind was already running imaginary Excel spreadsheets and calculating pros and cons, investment requirements and potential business models. My heart, though… Well, my heart just ached for feeling the *campo* under my feet. Argentina had hit me strongly and unexpectedly, and I simply could not help but go back there.

And then there were the people I had met. The family in the middle of the pampas that I had spent Christmas with: Patricio, the professional polo player I had trained with; Gabriela, his girlfriend; and their extended family. All the countless cousins and nieces and nephews, uncles and aunts I had met there. All those smiley and welcoming people. And among them a special figure: Rosario.

Argentines like nicknames, and Rosario's was Ro. I found that out pretty quickly. Ever since I had met her at the Christmas party, I knew she and I would be in touch for a very long time. She looked straight at me with a pair of dark brown eyes, the same shade as her dark brown hair, and beamed a wide smile even before we were introduced by the customary kiss on the cheek.

"Hi, I'm Rosario," she said in perfect English. I'm Patricio's cousin." By that time I had given up counting his cousins and figured out that everyone there would be some sort of cousin.

I felt warmth when I first spoke to her, as if inexplicably she and I had met before. I felt I already knew her. We drank Campari orange and talked all night, and then Gabriela joined us, and as the morning broke we decided to take a trip to the seaside.

Three days and many bottles of wine later, we returned bonded like sisters. She invited me to stay with her next time I was in Argentina, and I smiled and thanked her. Little did we know I would take up her invitation so soon.

So now as I break the news of my imminent return to Argentina over the phone, I can hear the shock in her voice.

"But, Roxy, what are you going to do here? Are you coming for polo?" she asks, still not fully believing I'm coming back so soon.

"Yes, I'll play some polo. Maybe. But not much. Listen, Ro, I want to set up a business. Maybe we can set up a business together!"

The enthusiasm in my voice could neither be faked nor hidden. She laughs.

"Sure, Roxy. That would be great. But I'm not sure what we can do. I'm an art teacher, remember?"

I remember. But I don't care. I must sort something out. Something that will enable me to stay there. Forever.

And so I went. This time I booked a flight with a return date two weeks later. I couldn't justify an open-ended flight. Not again. I told myself I had two weeks to make this dream a reality. Find something, anything that would allow me to live in Argentina.

Rosario picked me up from the airport, took me home, gave me lots of food and drink, and we had a good chat, and then she taught me the most important lesson about living in Argentina.

"Shall we start working on this business idea now?" I ask her immediately after lunch. "Look, I'm thinking of revisiting all the estancias where I was last time and proposing a deal. I'll market their services in England, get groups to come here to play polo, and you organize the logistics here, and they would pay us a commission… and I could even play polo for free!"

"Roxy!" she interrupts me. "There's nothing we can do right now. It's siesta time. We're going to sleep for a couple of hours, and then around four we wake up, have a *mate,* and then think about what we want to do."

And that was it. My quick intro into the Argentine lifestyle. No one moves between one and four in the afternoon; everybody has a siesta.

So, we have a siesta and then drink some *mate,* the official and omnipresent tea of the Argentines, made with *mate* leaves and shared from the same cup among friends. Then she listens to all my ideas again and offers a suggestion.

"Roxy, I think you need a boyfriend. How about the *bonbon* you met over Christmas at Emi's estancia? I think he was single. And pretty handsome."

The *bonbon*—Argentine for sweetie—she refers to is indeed exactly that: a sweetie. A tall, blond German polo player, and a surfer in his spare time, deliciously unaware of his sex appeal. Friendly, handsome, laid-back. In short, cool, really cool. And he plays polo professionally. What more could I ask? After our trip to the seaside the last time I was in Argentina, we stopped by one of the estancias I played polo at and there we met the said *bonbon*. He was a guest polo instructor there for the whole season. Likely he would still be there.

"How about we go back there? To Emi's estancia. We can talk to Emi about your business idea. And see if the *bonbon* is still there." I agree.

❧

One week and a number of estancias later, reality slowly takes hold of me. I've learned a lot more than I'd anticipated.

First, I learned that Rosario was a true friend as well as an Argentine, which made her a true Argentine friend. This meant a lot. True Argentine friends drop everything in their life at the shortest of notice to help their friends. She drove me around in her car, took time off work, and endured countless conversations where I brainstormed one business idea after another. She listened to everything, smiled at everything, taught me how to drink *mate*, and inevitably turned the conversation towards the boyfriend I was supposed to find and my lack of applied focus in this particular area of my life.

Second, I learned that not all business ideas necessarily materialize. Together we brainstormed and promptly discarded one idea after the other. I was usually the originator of the idea, and she was the rational mind pounding the last nail in the coffin. I didn't mind; after all, it was hard to argue with her rational approach. To her credit, she didn't mind my inventing a new idea just as she'd finished burying the previous one. We worked well as a team.

And third, I learned that the *bonbon* really was a sweetie. After an initial visit to Emi's estancia, where Emi, the owner, politely listened to my business idea, smiled, said nothing, and offered me some *mate*, I found another way to approach the *bonbon*. I booked some polo lessons with him. So I would come back every afternoon, have a lesson with him, and offer him the opportunity to chat me up. I thought this was a great plan. Rosario liked the *bonbon* too but wasn't sure the polo lesson path was the right approach. After a couple of lessons, it started to rain heavily—it turned out that Argentina experiences a mini rainy season in February—so our polo lessons were confined to a wooden horse in a cage, where I would relentlessly hit ball after ball under the careful guidance of the *bonbon* while Rosario patiently waited for me, hoping I would report some progress on the love side.

"Roxy, this is not going to work," she announces with a serious look in her eyes one day as I finish my polo lesson.

"What? The business idea? Listen, Ro, I know you're not convinced we'll find something, but I can feel it, it's in the air. We're going to find the right thing to do. I know we've been to all these estancias, and they weren't interested. But we will find something. Really. We just need to be patient, and it will come."

"No, Roxy, it's not about the business. It's about love. You need some love in your life, and you're really not going to find it like this!"

"What do you mean?" I ask, taken by surprise.

"Like this!" She points back to the wooden horse. "You are not flirting with this guy. I tell you. I've watched you carefully these last few days. He's a *bonbon*, and you need one. But like this there's no chance."

"What do you mean?" I ask again, confused.

"You interact with him completely non-sexually," she replies.

"Of course I interact with him completely non-sexually! I'm hitting polo balls on a wooden horse! How on earth would I interact with him sexually?"

"Roxy, do you like him?" she asks with a determined look.

"Yes, I do," I admit.

"Then why don't you show him you like him?" she says, frustrated.

"I do show him," I reply, equally frustrated. "I'm showing him enough. I'm coming here day after day in the rain to train with him on this wooden horse. Doesn't he understand?"

"No, Roxy." Rosario's voice has turned soft again. I detect a little pity in there. "He doesn't understand. All he sees is a client who pays him to learn to play polo. A very serious client focused on her polo hits."

"Well, I suppose that is what I am," I admit. "But I can be more…"

"But you don't *flirt*, Roxy! I've watched you, day after day. Not a single time have you flirted with him!"

Her voice has that hint of accusation again.

"It's kind of difficult," I say in my defense. "I really want to learn my hits, after all, so I need to focus on that too…"

"You have to decide. Focus on the polo balls or focus on his balls. Your choice."

I burst out laughing. Rosario could be very direct.

"And what if I want both?"

"You can have both of his balls. Or as many of the polo balls as you want. But they don't mix well together. It's either one or the other."

"Ro, you don't understand. We're polo buddies. I can't flirt with him so openly."

"Exactly," she concludes. "You said it so well."

We leave the conversation there, and I think about it long and hard. My mind is resisting, but my heart tells me she's right. Love or polo—will I really have to choose?

To Each Their Own

FEBRUARY

At least I tried, I told myself as I contemplated the approaching date of my return flight. I came here and tried to find a business. It didn't happen. I even tried to flirt with the *bonbon*. It didn't happen. I didn't meet anyone else either. The *campo* was pretty unfriendly as well, soaked wet under the thunderstorms that raged for days on end. No polo estancia was interested in my services. No polo player was interested in me.

"Very well. I'll go back home." I decided to accept defeat graciously. At least I still had polo.

So, to lift my spirits before going back, I booked myself into a polo estancia for twenty-four hours. A nice farewell treat. The rains had stopped, and it looked like we could finally play some polo. And with nothing else left to hang onto, I needed polo really badly.

I kissed Rosario good-bye and thanked her for her hospitality. She hugged me back, wished me good luck in my search for love, ignored my attempt to bring the conversation back to future business opportunities, and told me she hoped we would see each other again soon.

"*Mi casa es tu casa,*" she added. My house is your house. Exactly what an Argentine friend would say.

So I left the welcoming world of real Argentine friends and stepped into the world of commercial Argentine estancias for one more night, just before my flight back home. I played some practice chukkas and noticed my hitting was much better thanks to the countless shots under the careful guidance of the *bonbon*. I was pleased but not happy. I kept wondering if Rosario was right and if I was still single because I was incapable of flirting with a man. Or, worse still, if I was still single because I loved playing polo.

With these thoughts still on my mind, I take my towel and head towards the swimming pool. It's late afternoon, after the practice chukkas, and tomorrow I'll fly back home to the middle of the winter. I better enjoy a few hours in the pool while I can.

I find myself a sun lounger and glance at the handsome guy reading his book next to me. A polo player. I haven't played with him this afternoon, but I remember seeing him dressed for polo when I arrived. He's one of the polo guests, most probably.

He lifts his head out of his book and takes a glance at me. I can't see his eyes, hidden by dark sunglasses, but I can feel his look.

I remember Rosario's flirting advice. "Just smile," she'd said, "and look available. Carefree. Happy. Like a butterfly."

I try a smile. I can do this, I think. Can't do much about being carefree though. I care about a lot of things right now. Like my failed business plan, for a start. Can't say I'm really happy either. I have to go back home tomorrow, so what's to feel happy about? But I just played polo. This is good. Happy. Let's do happy. Polo happy.

I try to smile again.

Not good enough, I tell myself. I need to try harder. I smile again. Happy. I try to tell myself that I'm happy. Carefree. Like a butterfly.

"I saw you play this afternoon," he says, still looking at me from above his book.

My smile widens. Rosario would be proud of me. I smiled and it worked. A man, a polo player actually, initiated a conversation.

"So how come you play polo?" he says in a lazy voice.

I look at him and decide against my "reincarnated knight" story. Too long, too complicated, and not really suitable for flirting. What would be a flirtatious answer? I wish Rosario were here now.

"I like it." I go for the truth. Surely one can flirt and say the truth at the same time, no?

"Hmm, really?" his voice turned ironic. "It must be really good for you girls. Playing polo I mean. You have a good chance of meeting a rich husband, playing polo."

All of a sudden I feel the smile wiped off my face.

"What do you mean?" I ask, still wanting to give him a chance to prove he's just a nice guy trying to chat me up.

But he's not. He's just a bastard.

"All you girls in polo. Are you really playing because you love it or because you want to find a rich husband?" he repeats, this time the irony in his voice quite obvious.

I feel the rage building up in me. I don't even know why I'm so angry. It's true that I'm looking for someone. But not for a rich husband. I don't give a shit if he's rich or not. But he has to play polo. Does this mean I'm just playing polo because I'm looking for someone?

Screw him. I decide to turn his remark around. Treat people as they treat you, I remember the advice of a former boss of mine. When they attack you, attack them in the same way. This is where they are most vulnerable; that's why they choose that specific form of attack in the first place.

"How about you, then? Are you looking for a rich wife? One who can sponsor your polo, I mean?" I keep a straight face as I reply. I even try to match the irony in my voice to his.

He doesn't expect this, I can tell. The expression on his face turns to that of a lost child, and he decides to abruptly end the conversation and drops his gaze back to the book he's reading.

I close my eyes and pretend I'm sunbathing, but I'm still boiling with rage.

Polo prejudices. I'd heard them so often that soon I came to expect them, and when they came, I knew exactly how they sounded.

The most widespread one is that women who play polo are after sexy polo players. Not that it's not true. Sometimes. Most of the time. Well, for single girls, at least. But that isn't why we play. And to be honest, maybe Rosario was right. Maybe we girls who play polo can't find a boyfriend who plays polo precisely because we play polo.

It's enough to picture how a girl looks when she has just finished playing a four-chukka game, the sweat drenching her face, her hair, pulled in all directions, sticking out of her helmet. If she has make-up on, it's running all over her face. But most likely there's no make-up at all, just the dirt from a fall or two, or from trying to wipe her sweat away with a dirty polo glove. After the game, she stinks like a horse and walks with a limp, likely due to the bruises acquired during the game, bruises that will probably prevent her from wearing a miniskirt for the entire duration of a polo season.

The picture in my head becomes vividly real. It isn't a pretty one. I probably look like this after every game I play. Hmmm… not appealing to a guy. Really not. Perhaps I need to reconsider my approach. Some sweat-resistant make-up might help. And maybe a fresh pair of clothes to change into after every polo game. I could keep a mirror and a small make-up bag in my polo bag. There must be ways around this.

Then there's another prejudice, the same one my swimming-pool companion just voiced: Women who play polo are trying to find a rich husband. So it's either a hot date or a rich husband. Or ideally both. This is the one that irritates me most because it assumes women have no money of their own, and they must constantly try to get it from a man. It gives me the shivers, and when I hear it, I usually bite back. Just like I did to my unsuspecting sun-lounger neighbor. And it's also linked to the assumption that to play polo one must have a lot of money. It is so deeply ingrained in the public psyche that polo is a sport for the rich that they don't stop to think. I get asked this question by people I know and people I've just met. Under different circumstances, the same people would never dream of asking how much I earn or how much I spend, but with polo it seems like this is a perfectly acceptable topic of conversation.

My favorite answer is that it costs less than having a kid. This generally stops any follow-up questions. People are shocked. You can't think this way, they tell me. But they don't really want to discuss how much they spend raising a kid in London either, so the conversation suddenly and politely comes to an end.

I feel the sun of the late afternoon warming my face as my anger fades away. Tomorrow I go back to England, back to the cold. I didn't find my business here. I didn't even find my polo player. But at least I still have polo. And to hell with all this prejudice. I know my truth.

I am a girl who plays polo. Because I love it.

Playing Like a Girl

MARCH

I returned from Argentina empty-handed, with my business plan in ashes and still single. I swallowed my pride and my pain and went back to my polo club. It was still winter, and the only polo available was the muddy version in the arena, but I clung to it with the desperation of a drowning person clinging to a lifeline. At least I still had polo.

I played every weekend and sometimes during the week too. My hitting sessions with the tall blond *bonbon* had borne results, and my English trainers commented on my improved game. I told myself that not all was lost; at least I had become a better polo player in Argentina.

Rosario's words of advice about dating still played on my mind, and one day I decided to do something about it. I was battered and covered with bruises from the regular weekend games, and I felt my feminine self needed some urgent care. So I booked myself a "get in touch with your feminine essence" yoga workshop.

The following Saturday night, instead of putting on my high heels and sexy black dress ready to go out, I slipped into my yoga pants and headed over to my feminine connection workshop. There I met a lovely lady, chanting beautifully in Sanskrit the whole evening, and about twenty other women with whom I shared a relaxing evening of *asanas*, breathing exercises, gathering energy, visualizing, singing, and basically doing all sorts of things that not long ago I would have classified as wasting time. I forced myself to take it all seriously, and my self-hypnosis must have worked because I left feeling refreshed and soft, smiling at the world. I even felt I was in love with the whole world. Pure bliss!

The next day I went to play polo, and here the trouble started.

While the week before I had been told off for dangerous riding and being too aggressive after smashing my dearest friend into the boards while fighting for the ball, this week… well, this week it's a slightly different game.

I start by attempting to ride off someone. And that someone or something, either the guy I'm riding off, or his horse's head, or his mallet, something knocks off my helmet, and I continue riding, blissfully unaware, until they stop the game and pick up my helmet from the muddy arena. I have three guys fastening it securely onto my head to make sure it won't come off again, which says something about their confidence in my ability to fasten it myself. Then, a bit frightened by this initial ride-off, I try to be more gentle, until my coach starts shouting at me in an irritated voice:

"Roxy, what the hell are you doing? When I ride someone off it doesn't look like I'm kissing him!"

I don't have time to wonder what that was supposed to mean before I get shouted at again. Apparently I'm in the wrong place, or I'm carrying the stick the wrong way up (never happened before, I swear). Then, trying hard to keep the ball away from our goalpost, I manage a successful backhand shot, and I feel pleased to see the ball moving away, until I hear another shout:

"It's called a backhand because it's done with the back of the hand! What's that girly move?"

I realize I've hit the ball in a really awkward way, which is described as "shifting a handbag under your arm," and even though it did the job, it's seen as a big no-no by all those present.

Then I almost score a goal by hitting the ball into our own goalpost, and I hear my coach shouting again:

"Dude! The other way!"

Somehow, "dude" feels more surprising than the fact that I was about to score a goal against my own team. Dude? Does he mean me?

Some more headless-chicken running around, not quite understanding where I should be, but I have a lovely feeling of being in touch with the energy, and my body, and the sun on my skin. The woman chanting in Sanskrit would have been proud of me, really. She would have, but my coach is not, and I hear another shout: "Mate! What's wrong with you today?"

I looked around for the "mate" but, no, it's me again. Mate? Probably sensing my lack of response, my coach switches to my name, but his tone is still harsh:

"Wake up, Roxy! We're losing here, big time!"

Fortunately, I'm helped by a kind guy from the opposing team, who, instead of riding me off and stopping me from scoring a goal, rides gently by my side and encourages me.

"Come on, don't play the gentleman, ride me off for God's sake!" I shout. But no, he decides to look after me in the middle of the game, like a true gentleman would.

And the game carries on, with my coach swearing, and with me smiling at the sun, at the world, and at my horse, and feeling like I should be really gentle with him—the horse, I mean—so I don't push him or whip him, and this means everyone else is far ahead of me. And, no, I don't push anyone into the boards today either.

And after the game, there are no more grumpy comments from my coach, who comes to give me a hug instead. And I get smiles and kisses from all the other guys, which is rare in England, where people don't touch, don't kiss, and usually freak out if there's less than a foot separating them from another human being.

I have no idea what happened to me today, but someone please help me! My polo is going down the drain, and I think the woman chanting in Sanskrit has something to do with this!

The Old Man's Farm

My polo has reached a kind of "no man's land": too good to play with the polo school any longer but not good enough to play with the regular members of one of the top high-goal clubs in England, which I had decided to join. I am caught in-between, not sure how to go forward.

My headache is the headache of our club manager too, who has decided that for the first time he will put a special package out there for a few of us, the "in-betweeners." We can only play among ourselves, at certain times only, and under no circumstances mix with the "big guys."

I have trained with some of the best teachers in England, who taught me to ride and be safe on a horse. My balance is good, my half-seat still causes me lower back pain at times, but I manage to hold it long enough to do the job. My swing is clean. They kept on telling me all is "wonderful," "perfect," and "really nice." My game wasn't that good though. Then, I trained with some great Argentine professionals who told me to run, to look around, to get out there in the game and not worry so much about the details. A different approach. My English coaches didn't like that. "Back to basics," they said, and so I had to unlearn some of the Argentine ways and relearn some of the English ways. More confusion.

Lost in translation, I went on, like a camel crossing the desert, putting one foot in front of the other, lost in the midst of the dunes with a vague hope that I would find my way to the other side.

On my search, I arrived at the Old Man's farm. Only an hour's drive from London, I find myself back in Argentina. The *petiseros* get the horses ready, and among the familiar "Dale, Dale" shouts, I have a vague feeling that this might be the answer to my prayers. The middle ground between England and Argentina.

The Old Man rides next to me on the stick-and-ball field. He's silent, his expert movements swiftly guiding the horse. He must have spent many years on the back of a horse. He's seen it all and has no time for the "politically correct" approach of my English coaches. He doesn't look for something good to tell me, to encourage me. When it's bad, he says so plainly. "Rosannaaa! Ay ay ay, no no no, bad, bad!" adding at the end just for clarification, "*Not* good!," so I really get that it's not good.

Not a lot of what I do is any good anyway. After he lines up five balls for penalty shots, I take my horse in a wide circle canter and miss them all. Some I don't even touch. A smile appears on his face as if he's really enjoying the show.

"You want my glasses so you can see the ball better? Ay ay! Not good."

He lines them up again, and this time I hit a few. Maybe I'm too tired to care, so my body takes over from my over-controlling mind, and my shots improve. Some are really good shots, but I still miss the goal.

"That's better, isn't it?" I ask, hoping for some encouragement.

"Not good, not better at all. If it doesn't go through the goal, what's the use of a nice shot?" And so I decide there are no more questions from my side.

"Come, take the ball from me. Come on! Rosanna, what are you doing? Ay ay, you lost the ball. No, no, Rosanna, no swing like madwoman, look here, nice clean swing—like that!" I try to distance myself from the "madwoman swing," but I just miss more balls.

"Go e-straight! Faster, faster!" His heavy Spanish accent puts an *e* in front of any word that starts with an *s*. Eeee-straight! E-straight! I get him, but my horse doesn't want to go e-straight, or maybe he doesn't speak English. I canter around, bouncing from the left leg to the right leg, but the Old Man maintains a patient look in his eyes.

"Again! Go! Again, faster! Faster! Stoooop! Turn to the right! Faster! Offside hit! Run faster, faster!"

I have never gone this fast, at least not consciously while training. During the game it's another story, since only part of me is present to register how fast I go and get scared. The other part is lost somewhere else, usually ahead with the ball or lingering around the horse's heavy breathing. But here on the training field, it's just me and him and the gray English skies, which start squeezing out the first drops of rain this morning.

"Faster, faster. Run! E-straight! Stop! Turn to the left! Nearside shot! Run, faster!"

The horse is breathing heavily under me. I must have stopped breathing altogether. I feel the worrying sensation of an approaching faint as I do what the Old Man wants me to do again and again and again: run faster, stop, turn, hit, run faster, stop, turn, hit. After about twenty minutes of this mad run, my knees are finally about to give in. But the Old Man is merciless.

"Up in the saddle when you turn. Not like this, don't sit down, you are killing the horse. Up!" One more try and finally my knees give in. With my last ounce of strength, I bring the horse to a final stop.

"Wait… one moment… let me catch… my breath… this is really… difficult!"

His eyes are sharp, and he's no longer smiling.

"If it's too difficult, you should stay in London in front of your computer. Why bother coming all the way here?"

I hear the first drops of rain hitting my helmet. But it's OK. We're done for the day. And I'm done with my search too. Because with that one sentence, the Old Man has told me he's going to be the one to take my polo forward.

Polo Twins

MAY

A long time ago, under the stars of the savannah, a wise African man told me this: "Your problem is that you've got twins living inside you. One belongs to civilization and all those posh things: your job, your studies, your life in your big and busy city, and all the social status you're after. The other one brings you here to the savannah and shouts out its own story about adventure and exploration, about nature and wilderness. The problem is the first one was born just ten minutes before the second one, and she claims her right as "firstborn". You live by the rules she dictates, and you go ahead and build your life in the direction she takes you, and you try hard not to hear the second one, whose shout is now no more than a whisper. There will come a time when you will not be able to ignore that whisper any longer."

I left the wise African man in his wilderness and came back to Europe and went about my life back home but, even now, eleven years later, his words still ring true.

My first twin plays polo at Club Posh. Here dogs are leashed and whites are pure white. The grass is immaculately kept, which means the fields are closed every time it rains heavily. We have a long list of rules and regulations and a beautiful clubhouse where I sip a Campari orange after the game while chatting to my friends.

At Club Posh no one mixes with the grooms. You do not tack or untack your own horse. The horses are presented to you on the polo field, all kitted out: you jump on, you jump off. That's it. Then the grooms take them away, and you have no idea what happens behind the scenes.

Club Posh has beautiful tournaments where people arrive by helicopter, and luxury car manufacturers compete to display their valuable goods. Club Posh is where I linger in the evenings, listening to music under the huge safari-style tent with comfortable sofas, watching kids play in the grass with polo balls and foot mallets.

Club Posh is where I started playing polo by a twist of fate and a meeting of two dogs on the streets of London. It was here that I fell in love with the game, and it was love at first sight, that first day, in the mud of the arena and in the rain.

My second twin plays polo at Club Real. Here grooms call horses *hermano* (brother), and people care. They really care about you and your polo, about your progress, and they push you hard and make you touch the edges of your limits. Club Real, a country club with a strong Argentine feel, is where I really learned to play polo. After sixteen months of carefully and slowly trying out things at Club Posh, I made a huge leap forward at Club Real.

"Dale, dale! *Cola, cola!*" Club Real is where I learned to talk to my teammates, to shout like them, in their language, to loosen up the stiffness I had acquired at Club Posh, to become real, to have genuine fun in a game. To have fun after the game, too, as I pull the tail of a horse trying to undo the very tight braid while the grooms laugh their heads off and call me *Petisera*…

Club Real is where I relax and have a friendly chat over a Sunday *assado*. It is here where I can be myself, my true and authentic self, my second twin whose whisper has finally found its voice.

I arrived at Club Real by chance, one Saturday morning, for a lesson with the Old Man. Since then, I've felt part of the family. Here my love at first sight for the game deepened into a passion for life. And maybe this was the answer to my prayers: I couldn't find a way to stay in Argentina, but Argentina came to greet me here, in England. I found the unmistakable Argentine friendliness at only a fifty-minute drive from central London.

And somewhere between these two clubs, only twenty miles but a world apart, my heart smiles and sings as it greets my twins who are slowly but surely going their separate ways…

Conversations with a Horse

MAY

The wind is blowing like a mad hurricane. The horses are nervous; I don't think they like that wind at all. It's the first game of the season, and they are fresh and scared. Our coach doesn't make things any easier as he tells us right before the first chukka, "Guys, ride like you mean it! The horses might be a bit fresh today."

This is an understatement. The horses are mad, not fresh. Already, in the first two minutes of the chukka, it becomes very clear that the dark brown mare and I are not seeing eye to eye today.

"Leeeft! Go to the left!" I hear the faraway cry of one of my teammates.

I know what he means. Another player in my team is ahead and he's preparing to do a backhand. I know exactly where the ball is going to go, but there's no way I can persuade my horse to go there.

"Leeeft! Left, I said!" I hear the shout again. "That was right!"

I know. My horse has decided to go right instead and there's not much I can do. Whatever I want to do, she thinks differently. I ride on and pull the reins. She doesn't stop. I pull harder. Harder. I pull until I feel my fingers squeezed and about to break. The only thing I achieve is that the mare now bounces nervously on both front legs. I start losing my balance. I really don't like what's going on.

The game has moved on at the other side of the field while I carry on my argument with the horse.

"Roxy, what the heck are you doing there?" the captain of my team shouts across the field.

I don't answer. What can I say? That I suddenly lost all my riding skills?

One of my former coaches is the umpire in this game. I ride around him in circles, begging him to help me. The mare doesn't want me on today, it's clear.

"Roxy, move on, I can't help you," the coach says. "I need to umpire this game! I can't do that with you riding in circles around me!"

"I'm gonna get thrown off!" I shout back in desperation as the mare gets more and more angry with me. I start to panic.

"Just give her some rein! Look, you've locked her head, and she can't move! Just give her some rein and she'll calm down!"

I'm too scared to give her rein. I don't trust this horse to calm down. I'm afraid she'll run wild with me, and I won't be able to stop her. So I pull tighter, she bounces more strongly, and now I lose my stirrups. As if by magic my legs have become shorter, and I can no longer reach my stirrups. Much later on, I learn that fear makes the body contract, and the muscles get shorter; hence the stirrups get longer. I didn't know it then, and even if I did, it wouldn't have helped me. Nothing and no one could possibly have helped me at that moment.

The game goes on in the distance while I fight with my horse alone. From under my Oakley protective glasses, my tears start falling one by one, thankfully blown dry by the wind. I am now crying on a polo field.

As the chukka comes to an end and I jump off, I declare I never want to see that horse again. I'm shaking in my boots, but I dry my eyes, bite my lip, and with a trembling hand I pull the reins of my next horse. But guess what? My next horse turns out to be another devil. Another chukka clinging to its back like my life depends on it. Another argument with another horse. By now I am convinced there's something irremediably wrong with my riding skills. Either that or all the horses have gone mad today. Things get worse. The third horse doesn't listen either. By the time I get on the fourth one, I have absolutely no expectation that it will be any better. And I'm right.

I rode four devils that day and never touched the ball. When the game was over, I felt it was a miracle that I was still alive.

I needed a full week to recover after that game. I wasn't sure what hurt the most. The grip of panic as I felt I was about to be thrown off? The desperation of fighting with an animal who's a ton heavier than me? The jokes of my teammates about my rapidly deteriorating riding skills? Seeing the same horses, which were so out of control with me, being so docile when ridden by other people? No idea. Hurt and humiliated, I thought that maybe I had arrived at the limits of my polo.

Something had to change. Either that or I had to give up the game.

It was then I remembered the words of one of my early polo coaches: "Think like a horse! Always ask yourself, what does the horse want? What does he see? What does he feel? And remember, there's one thing on his mind. He is a prey animal and he wants to stay alive. And he has to trust you and know that if he does what you say, he will survive…"

Think like a horse. The key was here. Think like a horse. The following weekend I started to experiment.

"I'll keep you safe," I told the horse as soon as I jumped into the saddle. "I promise I'll keep you safe."

And then I remembered a yoga grounding practice: I imagined

I was sending roots from my bum in the saddle through the horse's body and down his legs into the earth: long, strong roots binding us together, the horse and me. "I'll keep you safe," I whispered to him again, watching his ears nervously moving around. I was sure he had heard me.

The first chukka went well. The horse was docile and listened to all my commands. Encouraged, I tried the same approach with the second horse. Conscious of the presence of the other players around me and not really wanting to risk being overheard in my conversations with the horse, I didn't whisper this time. I promised him I'd look after him in my own mind. His ears still moved just as I thought the words. In a weird kind of way, it felt as if he'd heard my thoughts.

That game was one of the most peaceful I'd ever had. I wasn't sure if it was because of that little trick of growing roots and sending them into the earth through the horse's legs, or if it was because of my promise to him. But the horse and I became one body. He obeyed me gently and naturally; he trusted me, and I trusted him. I grew more confident and more relaxed. I worried less about the horse and more about the ball. My game improved.

I have never fought with a horse since. I just talk to them in a whisper or sometimes in my own mind. It's our thing, our ritual, our little conversation as we walk forwards to line up for the start of a new chukka. And the movement of their ears tells me they hear me, every time.

"I'll keep you safe, I promise," I tell them. "Just play with me."

The miracle happens again: they do. And we play. Together.

<h1 style="text-align:center">More Early</h1>

JUNE

These days I train with Cholo at Club Real. After a few unanswered questions, I gave up trying to understand what his nickname really means and just call him *Cholo* as all the others do. He is a young Argentine professional polo player who plays polo like a god. He doesn't talk much though. Only the occasional instruction shouted across the field in the heat of the game. When I train with him, he's even quieter. He just takes his horse silently to the stick-and-ball field, and without a word he hits the first ball as we get there. I know what this means. I get my horse into a canter in front of him and go towards the ball. If I miss it, he will hit it at me again. And then again and again. Until the hour is done, the horses out of breath, and I'm clinging to the saddle more dead than alive.

He plays amazing polo, and I'm hoping to find out his secret, to learn how to do things right. I am hoping he will tell me something that, as if by magic, will correct my bad moves and make me a better player.

We hit more balls. I hit balls in silence with him riding behind, and I daren't stop for fear I'll hear his shout—"Move on!"

At Club Posh I trained with some top English coaches. They all told me what to do and what not to do: "Knees in, heels down." I was shouted at countless times as I learned to ride. "Legs an inch towards the back! No, no, not like that, that is too much, just an inch!" "Your swing is wrong, your elbow should be there, your finger should be pointing there, your other shoulder should be dropping here."

All very precise instructions that I tried to follow to the letter. It took a long time and many lessons. I was continually missing the ball as I concentrated on where my shoulder should be, what my finger should be doing, and whether my heels were low enough or in a perfect line with my hips and shoulders. Polo became a game of exact, precise positions. Do this, don't do that. If you do it exactly as I tell you to do it, you will hit the ball, I promise!

I came to expect this, someone telling me what to do. But here I don't get it. Except for the merciless shout "Move on!" when I slow my canter down or dare to stop, Cholo doesn't tell me anything else, neither when I hit well nor when I miss.

"Why don't you tell me what I'm doing wrong?" I ask, out of breath and full of frustration.

His eyes are serious. He looks at me, one long, tough stare, and shrugs his shoulders.

"Because it's useless. What do you want me to tell you? How I do it? It's not important for you. You have to find out how you do it yourself. You have to feel the ball as if the ball is a part of you. And only then will it go where you want it to go."

"And how do I do that?" I ask again, feeling my frustration bubbling up almost into tears.

"You just hit more balls," comes the answer.

I feel tears coming dangerously close. I am trying hard, so hard, and I feel I'm getting nowhere. In my mind I'm still expecting someone to help me, someone to tell me how to do it right, as if I'm not able to find my way on my own.

He probably senses how close I am to tears, and the look in his eyes softens in kindness. He nods his head towards the green field shining in the morning sun.

"Come on! Let's hit some more balls," he says as he breaks into a canter. "There's no shortcut to this. You need to hit enough balls so that you start to feel them."

I ride on behind him and this time I don't expect any advice.

Later that week, I attend a business leadership course. A former professional tennis coach, famous worldwide for his unique leadership program called "The Inner Game," shares with a group of top managers the secret to leadership, one that he has been researching his entire life. The secret that will make top executives better leaders.

"Never tell people how to do something. Let them find their own way. In business, as in tennis, the best results are achieved when you let yourself feel the ball inside you. It's the inner game as opposed to the outer game. Win your inner game first and the outer game will follow."

And then I get it: this well-known leadership coach for top executives and my polo coach are saying one and the same thing.

The following weekend I turn up to the polo field for my regular appointment with Cholo, and this time I don't expect anything: no instruction, no secret, and no shortcut. I have my inner game to play. I understand that finally, as clearly as I understand that the best thing he could have done for me is precisely what he is doing: letting me figure out my own connection with that ball.

We ride in silence for one hour, hitting balls. Sometimes I miss them, other times I hit them. Sometimes they go where I expect them to go, and at other times they decide to surprise me. I don't mind that any longer. I am here to learn their language.

And as we come to the end of that long and silent stick-and-ball session and get the horses to walk leisurely towards the stables, Cholo turns to me, his deep blue eyes looking steadily into mine, and smiles. "More early," he says.

"What?"

"Your swing, I mean. Try more early. You are missing balls because sometimes you're too late to swing."

I'm speechless. Just as I expected no more instruction, a little bit of help has just arrived.

I look back at him, a long, deep stare as if I expect him to tell me more. But he doesn't. He just smiles, nods his head again, places the mallet under his knee against the saddle and, with his right hand now free, lights himself a cigarette.

The horses are quickening their steps as if they're happy to go back to the stables. They're tired, but today's work is done for them. I'm tired too. But my work is not yet done. Somewhere at the back of my mind, my memory plays back my shots again and again. And as the feeling of hitting that ball settles into my subconscious, it mixes with the only bit of instruction I've received that day, which makes it even more memorable: more early.

I turn towards Cholo, who's lost in savoring his cigarette. I don't say anything, but I'm filled with gratitude. Not so much for the instruction, even though I really appreciate the hint. I'm filled with gratitude for the way he's giving me the space and the silence to find my own way.

Stick to Your Man

JUNE

"Talk to me! Talk to me, I am your teammate! Talk to me!"

His face is serious, borderline angry. I'm angry too, but for different reasons. I'm angry at the guy I was marking from the other team, who's decided to use this chukka as a platform to show off his polo skills. I'm angry because I'm not as good as he is, and I lose every ride-off. I'm angry because we're losing the game. I'm angry at myself for being angry. And now, he's angry too. We're riding back after the first chukka, and Cholo, who's the professional player on our team, is seriously pissed off at me.

"Talk to me, Rosanna! Talk to me! This is what teammates are for! When you see me with the ball, and you are behind, tell me if I should send it tail or open. I cannot see behind. I have to rely on you. Talk to me, OK? Talk to me!"

He has a point. I've never been too good at teamwork. But here on the polo field, you can only play as a team. There's no game for lonely riders. I nod my head in agreement. All right, I'll talk to you, I promise him silently in my own mind. The anger is still there as I change my pony, as I get on my new horse, and as I ride back to the field. I'm angry at my own anger.

But promises made in the surreal quiet time between two chukkas are hard to keep on the field. When the adrenaline kicks in, and the horses are running wild, your mind goes still, and any thoughts you hold fade away. You are left face to face with the raw you, the very naked raw you as you happen to be that day. And for me, today, I am left face to face with anger. I ride with anger, and I don't even notice that my horse feels my anger too, and he starts bouncing from one leg to the other and refusing to stop, refusing to turn…

"Rosanna! Stick to your man! Stick to your man!" I hear the shout of my teammate in the distance.

He's got no idea, but this is a tricky one for me. I'm still single: there's no man in my life to stick to. He means the man on the field, of course, the man I'm marking. But this is enough to get me angry once again, angry that a guy on a polo field reminds me that I've been single for some time now, angry that polo – the perfect substitute for having a relationship – is becoming a platform for sticking-to-your-man discussions. I ride on, irritated, forgetting about who I'm to mark, forgetting to talk to my Argentine teammate, forgetting about everything, even the ball and the game. I am back to dwell in anger.

"Stick to your man, I said!" his shout comes back, merciless.

"Not that one, Rosannaaaa! That one is not your man, the other one is your man, the one with the blue hat. Rosanna, you are confused! The other one, I said! Yes, that one! Stick to him. Don't lose him. This time you must not lose your man!"

No, he's not making fun of me. He's simply playing the game.

I get confused. I find a man I think is mine. It turns out he's the wrong man. Then I try to repair my mistake quickly before he shouts at me again, and I choose another one to mark, the first one who crosses my path. But no, this one isn't my man either. Alone and confused, I give up on men altogether and I ride around in circles on my own until Cholo shouts one more time.

"The blue hat, I said. Find the one in the blue hat. Number four!"

So number four must be the right one. I cannot see any blue hat on the field though. I look hard. Cholo has started speaking Spanish. I'm useless with his instruction anyway, and he's probably given up on me.

I find my blue-hat man, then I lose him again and get more dating advice from Cholo. I try hard to stick to my man, to talk to my teammate, and to remember there's a ball in the game as well. I try hard to do it all. I fail, get angry once again, and decide not to talk to anyone any longer.

"Rosanna, you put your head down, you don't look right, you don't look left, you just run, run, run. What type of game is this? Stick to your man, remember? And look at me, look where I am and talk to me, OK? Talk to me."

In the silence of the three minutes between the chukkas, I make another promise to myself. I'll accept the anger that is in me today. I'll simply let it be there and play through it. And then, once I do that, I'll find my man and stick to him.

The bell is ringing, and we line up on the field for the start of a new chukka, like a new blank page where the future is yet to be written. I line up next to Cholo, my mallet down, ready for the throw-in. I'll talk to him this time, I know I will…

Just Play the Game

JUNE

Monday evening I have a standing appointment with Morgan, my chiropractor. He's a fun guy, Morgan, and he chats a lot while he sticks needles into my muscles and finds all sort of mysteriously painful places to pull or press. There's no man who knows my body better than Morgan. A session with him involves a great deal of pain but is nevertheless a pleasure.

"Your left shoulder is a bit out of order today."

He doesn't need to say a word. I'm screaming as he pulls my arm in a contorted position behind my back.

"Yes, that's because I had a horse that was a bit hard in the mouth."

"But your right shoulder looks pretty good," he adds, unimpressed by my explanation.

I sigh.

"Yes, that's because I didn't really hit any balls in that game."

Sadly, this summarizes my current level of polo. I can ride, and I've learned to talk to the horse. I've also learned to listen to the ball on the stick-and-ball field. But in a game, I cannot hit that ball.

The Old Man has tried everything: patience, shouting, anger, even occasional encouragement.

"Rosanna! I don't understand. Your swing is perfect when there is no ball, but when you try to hit the ball, it goes all wrong, like you don't want to hit it! Rosanna, why don't you want to hit that ball?"

I tried hard. I got angry. It didn't work. I missed it every time, and with each miss I became even more angry. It looked like it was mocking me, lying there still on the field, and I got my horse to run past it; then I turned around and tried again and again. It was still there, inert in the middle of the field, lying there peacefully, smiling at me, enjoying watching my useless trials.

And during the game, it got even worse. I missed it most of the time. With the kick of adrenaline, another player riding me off and the horse going fast, far too fast for me, I missed the ball again and again.

I tried everything. I tried not thinking about it, pretending it didn't exist. I still missed it. Then I focused on it so hard that it felt like my whole universe was reduced to the size of that ball. I missed it again. I got angry at it and missed it even more.

It's not fair, I told myself. Some huge, mysterious plot was afoot, and they were all against me: the ball, the team I was playing against, and even my teammates, who managed so successfully to hit it while I continued to miss.

"It's not important," my teammates tried to encourage me. "You played well, you marked well, you helped someone else score. It's teamwork, remember? It doesn't matter that you didn't touch the ball."

But it did to me. It mattered a lot, and the more it mattered, the less I hit it.

And then, suddenly, I got it. The memory of a game I saw in Argentina came back to my mind in full force. It was a game like many others, with good riders and fast horses. Only in this game, one team was clearly discriminated against by the umpire. Whistle after whistle he stopped the game and awarded penalties to the other team, most of them undeserved. It became so obvious that people watching at the edges of the field were soon swearing at the umpire, getting angry, getting agitated. But the very odd thing was that the players who were being unjustly treated didn't get angry. They came to change ponies and commented that yes, indeed, the umpire was unfair to them. But the incredible thing that struck me was that they didn't seem angry. It was just part of life: They had a game to play, and they were going to play it to the best of their abilities, no matter what else was happening on the field.

The memory of that game stayed with me long after it was over. Their detachment, their determination to play the game as it came, fair or not. Their decision to go back on the field chukka after chukka and simply do their best. Their willingness to keep on playing regardless of the circumstances. And the really strange thing was that in the end, they actually won the game. Had they become angry about what was going on, their game would have started to deteriorate. But no, they kept cool, they played their best, and they won despite the odds.

Eight months later and two continents away, the memory of that game hit me suddenly, on my English polo field in the middle of my struggles with the ball.

"It's not important," I told myself. "Let's see how it feels if I just play my best, whatever my best is at the time. If they could play so coolly with an umpire who clearly favored the other team, well, I can play my best against a ball that refuses my shots."

As soon as I took the pressure off, my shots improved, but I didn't even notice for a while. I was busy being in the game, playing the game, whatever that meant at the time, whether it was about marking someone or riding off or hooking or leaving the ball to my teammates. I was busy playing the game, playing like nothing else mattered. And only then did the ball start to play with me too.

And this is when I fully realized one of the most important lessons polo has ever taught me:

When the umpire throws the ball in and says "play," you play. You don't judge whether it's right or wrong, good or bad, fair or not. You simply… play.

Don't Touch That Ball!

JULY

"Leave it!" he shouts, just as I'm about to hit the ball. "Don't touch the ball!"

I let my mallet swing just above the ball and ride on, helplessly looking on as a guy from the other team takes it. Why? Why did he tell me not to hit the ball?

It's the third time in this game that Cholo has told me to "leave it." For one reason or another, he's not happy for me to hit the ball, even when I'm in the best position to do so.

Confused and irritated, I ride towards him at the end of the chukka and ask him why.

"Because you fouled!" Once again his face is serious. Cholo is usually very serious on the polo field. "Come on, Rosanna, you should know this by now! When you cross the line, speeding in front of a guy from the other team, you cannot touch the ball before they do, or you are in foul!"

Yes, I now remember the rule from the *Blue Book*. Only I had no idea I was crossing the line.

"You hurry all the time. You don't look. You cross the line. And then you want to take the ball. You cannot touch it, remember! You cannot touch that ball after you cross the line! You want to do too much, that's why you're fouling!"

For a split second I remember one of my other coaches at Club Posh telling me the same thing in different words. "You would play so much better if you would just relax a little!"

But I can't relax. Not in the middle of the game anyway, with my adrenaline pumping. I want to play, and I want to play well. And I want it now!

We go back to the field. I try to bear in mind the line of the ball and the rule of precedence, but I forget. Once again I cross the line, try to take the ball and get shouted at again. "Leave it! I said don't touch that ball!"

I heard it so many times during that game that, by the end of it, I thought maybe it held a bigger message for me. Maybe I should take a break from polo. It's the middle of the season now, and I've been doing too much, far too much. My twice-a-week routine had increased at an alarming rate: I was now playing chukkas Wednesdays and Fridays at Club Real, on the weekend at Club Posh, and in addition I showed up for my regular stick-and-ball sessions with Cholo or the Old Man at least once a week. Polo had managed to push everything else out of my life. Driving myself too hard, too fast, I was crossing my own internal line, and I was hardly aware of it.

So, I decided to take a break. I got on a plane and checked into a beach hotel in Mallorca. I didn't think much about where to go; I just browsed last-minute deals and found this island. I'd never been there before. I went alone because there were no friends to go with—my polo fiends wouldn't dream of going away during polo season, and my non-polo friends… well, with all the polo I was playing, I saw less and less of them. And I still had no boyfriend. But I decided not to worry about going somewhere alone. I could still have a nice time, I told myself. So I relaxed, fried on the beach, read novels, and swam in the sea. I realized it had been eleven months since I'd last swum in the sea.

Two novels and four days later, I felt reborn. With a nice tan and plenty of sleep, I felt I had enough distance from my polo passion. I was also done with lying on a beach alone. Since there was no mysterious Mr. Right trying to chat me up, I reverted to plan B: back to polo.

I come back. I go stick and ball. All goes fine. Then I play a game, and because it's the weekend, this one is at Club Posh. Games at Club Posh have become easy for me now that I play at Club Real at least twice a week. Club Real is where real polo happens. Club Posh is just a nice, protected environment where, under the umbrella of the "polo school membership", you're encouraged to play for fun but are never really ridden off by someone more experienced, never really hooked. Club Posh is where I play because I want to enjoy a nice drink afterwards with my friends.

The game goes well. I feel secure in the saddle, strong, invincible. I talk to my horses, and they listen to me. I send love to the ball, and it goes where I want it to go. I mark a far more experienced player, and I do it well. I feel this is all too easy for me, and I realize I'm actually looking forward to playing at Club Real again.

And then, in the last two minutes of the last chukka, the ball is sent ahead by a powerful hit. I ride on fast, in full gallop across the field with a rider from the other team next to me. It's going to be the last few shots of this game, I think, as I expect to hear the ring of the bell that marks the end of the game any minute.

But I don't hear the bell. Instead, I feel my horse suddenly disappearing from under me. In a fraction of a second, in the middle of my full gallop, the horse's head is no longer there. It's taken a dive onto the ground. And I dive too. A sudden jerk out of the saddle, a long flight over the horse's head and I land sharply on my right shoulder. As I hit the ground, I hear a distinct *crack* sound from under my shoulder blade.

Something must be wrong here is my last thought before the agony of pain takes over.

I didn't know it then but something was indeed wrong. I had broken both arms.

From Polo Girl to Barbie Doll

AUGUST

I feel my eyelids still heavy with sleep. I am somewhere in a borderline world between sleep and waking. My body takes over, trying to stretch into the familiar early morning movement that usually gets me out of bed. But a sharp pain in my right shoulder stops the stretch and brings me back to reality. I am lying on my back in bed with two broken arms. My right shoulder blade is broken in two places and held together by a muscle that has now become as hard as rock. There's no need for a cast, the doctors said, but I shouldn't move my arm. "Keep it in the sling and do not move it for at least six weeks."

My other arm is covered in a huge bandage. It's still numb, and I'm grateful. I have a low pain threshold, and I'm not particularly looking forward to the moment when the post-surgery numbness is gone and I'll start feeling again the place where they inserted two screws into my left wrist: the scaphoid bone and the radius. In addition to those two, there were a number of other fractures in my wrists and palm, too many and too small for the doctors to bother with. But at least these other ones didn't need screws.

It's only my second week of this new and unexpected routine. I lie in bed most of the day. When I'm not in bed, I'm on the sofa. I can't do much. My left hand is totally useless. I can use my elbow, though, and it comes in very handy for tasks such as closing a window. I can't use my right arm, which needs to stay stuck to my body, but I can grab things with my right hand. And with one elbow and one hand functional, life is not all that bad. After an accident like this, one gains a new perspective.

I lie in bed until my nanny rings the front-door bell. After the initial shock of learning I had broken both arms and being discharged from the hospital back home, where I live alone, I had to figure out a solution pretty quickly. Luckily, Girlie was with me all the way the day I fell. She was riding a dozen feet behind me, and she jumped off her horse and immediately ran to my side. She took me to the hospital and stayed with me for the seven hours of medical investigations that followed. And when she heard I was to be discharged and I'd be at home with two broken arms and no one to help me out, she made a number of frantic phone calls and she found a solution: a nanny.

So I have a nanny now, as if I have suddenly become a toddler again. She comes in every morning. We have a coffee together, after which she showers me, dresses me, tidies the place up, does some shopping, and prepares my meals for the rest of the day. Then she goes, and I'm left with just myself and my non-functional arms. Until the next day when she comes again.

The days pass. The six weeks become five, then four. I find things to do. I learn to enjoy my solitude. I learn to live again, without arms and without polo. I'm still not sure which one is harder to bear.

I get a phone call from Ziggy's dad, the man who got Girlie and me into polo on that fateful winter morning more than a year and a half ago. He tells me of his own polo accidents, of his own hospital encounters. Of how he put all that behind him and how he still enjoys playing polo, despite it all. And then he tells me:

"And you know, the most important thing to remember is that you were doing something you loved. When I ended up in the hospital in Switzerland after this game and I had a broken elbow and I had to stay there for a few days, I got told something that really touched me. The day I was discharged from the hospital, the nurse told me I should be happy that I got my injuries doing something I really loved. The guy next to me in hospital broke his leg falling off a ladder. A lady broke her arm while hanging out her washing. The hospital was full of people who had broken bones in the silliest ways imaginable. At least I'd been playing polo!"

His words are still with me every time I go to see my doctors for a check-up. I ask the other patients in the waiting room, "What happened to you?" I hear how they broke bones walking down the street, sliding on wet floors in supermarkets, or falling off their chairs. I hear of all sorts of incredible ways in which people break bones. At least I'd been playing polo.

No matter how good I feel about the reason why I broke my arms, though, it doesn't change reality: I'm helpless. Like a Barbie doll, I need to be washed, combed, dressed, and fed. After a few months of wearing only white polo jeans, I'm now wearing only dresses. It's the one item of clothing that can be pulled onto my body in the least painful manner.

Two weeks into this new "life after polo" routine, I feel I miss polo more than I miss my arms. I decide to go watch a polo game, one of the big games of the season. After I get my nanny to dress me, a friend comes to fetch me, and off we go. I can't play, but at least I can watch. It feels strangely familiar to be back on the side of a polo field. I watch the game with no resentment. And just as I'm walking back towards the car park with my friend after the game, I hear a shout coming from a long distance away:

"Rosannaaa!"

I turn around. It's the Old Man. I can see him in the distance, running towards me. Keeping my right arm in the sling and my left arm up in its bandage, I turn around and run towards him too. Since my accident happened at Club Posh, this is the first time he's seen me like this.

"Rosanna, what happened to you?" he says, catching his breath.

I smile. "Polo." There's nothing else to say.

"I know," he says. "Me too: got screws in my leg. Broke it badly last year."

I didn't know he had screws in his leg.

"But don't worry. You'll be OK. And you'll go back to polo. I'll get you back on a horse, you'll see."

"The season will be over before I'll be able to ride a horse," I say.

"Don't worry. Come to Argentina. I'll get you back on a horse, I promise," he repeats, his eyes looking straight into mine. I feel the weight of his promise.

There's not much else to say. I continue my walk towards the parked car. Another six hundred feet and I hear another shout:

"Rosanna!"

This time it's Cholo, who has also spotted me from a distance.

"What happened to you?" he asks as he runs towards me. He hadn't heard my conversation with the Old Man.

"Polo." Once again, there's no need to say anything else.

His eyes are serious, the same serious look he has on the field as we train together, the same serious look he has when he comes to talk to me between chukkas when we play together.

"Come to Argentina. Rosanna, come to Argentina. I'll get you back on a horse, I promise."

I nod. A brief Argentine kiss on the cheek and I disappear into my friend's car, which takes me all the way back to London. With me, I carry a double promise. One or both of them will get me back on a horse, I know that for sure. And the warmth in my stomach tells me that I've met people who really care.

I go home, and the memory of that day soon disappears into the monotonous "no arms" routine. Days drag by slowly. My nanny comes, and we have coffee. With her help, I take a shower. I get dressed, we chat, she goes. I read, I surf the web, I watch movies. I call my friends, and they come to visit. During the day, I do everything possible to find 1,001 things to keep me occupied.

But the nights… the nights are different. At night, I run away to a different place, somewhere green and spacious and airy where I can smell them and I can touch them again. Somewhere I can fly with them.

At night, I dream of horses.

Every Screw Has Its Screwdriver

SEPTEMBER

His face is serious. He's not joking. In the most serious way possible, he tells me that the screws in my wrist have displaced a small bone fragment and, to fix this, I will most likely need further surgery.

He's my cousin, the head of the orthopedic department of a top hospital. He fixed my knee many years ago when I tore it skydiving. I know he will help me if he can. But he says he can't do anything for my wrist.

"I can't take the screws out for you," he repeats. "We don't use these screws here. I haven't got a screwdriver for them. You need to go back to the surgeon who fixed them, and have him take them out."

He means the same surgeon who fixed them badly in the first place. The words sink deep into my stomach. It's been seven weeks since my surgery, and I still can't move my wrist.

Later that evening, I'm trying to forget about my wrist and the prospect of another operation with the help of a cocktail and a chat with an old friend.

"Roxy, look." Her voice is soft, her right arm lightly touching my frozen left wrist. "Have you ever thought that… well, this polo passion of yours. Have you ever thought that maybe you've become addicted?"

Addiction? This has crossed my mind before. I was warned by one of my first polo coaches at Club Posh. "Be careful with polo. It can easily turn into an addiction. It ends up sucking out your money and your life until you've got nothing left." I dismissed the comment immediately. It could happen to others, I thought. But not to me.

Then, after my fall, I met another friend in London who delivered the same message in a far less kindly way. "This is addiction! Look what you did to your body!" He pointed to my hands, one in a sling and the other wrapped in bandages. "Isn't this enough? And you're talking about wanting to go back to playing polo! Listen, there's an AA group meeting in this neighborhood. I think you should go there. You need some help to get out of this. You're addicted!"

I laughed it off. He was a very eccentric guy anyway, my friend, and when he told me that "people like you keep hospital beds from others who truly need them" I laughed even more. I thought he was nuts.

And now, the same message from another friend, delivered in a soft voice and with caring eyes. She's a trained physiologist. I can't ignore what she's talking about any longer.

"Roxy, come on, be honest with yourself. How much has polo taken from you? Not only the use of your arms, but how much money, how much time?"

I don't want to think about how much money or time. A lot. But it's not only that. I haven't worked for over sixteen months now. It's the longest break I've had in all my working life. This had nothing to do with polo, I'd told myself many times. I'm a freelancer, and work comes and goes. But now, this evening, in front of this cocktail, I remember a certain phone conversation I had in July some two weeks before my fall.

"Thanks, mate, for thinking of me for this project but really, seriously, I can't do it."

He paused, and then I heard him make one more attempt:

"You're joking, right? This is a good project. It's what you do, it's a company turnaround. It's perfect for you. You can't refuse it just because it's too far away from your polo club."

"Sorry, mate," I repeated. "I can't go to Manchester. Not now, not in the middle of the polo season. As crazy as it sounds, that's the reason I'm saying no."

I refused work. I refused to go out. I even forgot about my original intention: to meet Mr. Right. I was busy with polo, which slowly took over all my available time. All my available cash. When I wasn't riding, I was studying polo rules, watching polo videos, reading polo magazines. I sometimes went to birthday parties and social events rather reluctantly and spent a few hours drinking water and lemon because I had to go home and get a good night's sleep to be ready for the game in the morning. I postponed seeing friends. I refused to go out for dinners. I didn't book holidays. Week after week, my polo addiction was becoming stronger. It was the middle of the season.

Sometimes a distant thought crossed my mind: I have to stop this. I'm playing too much polo. But as soon as it came, I pushed it down, down so deep that I couldn't retrieve it easily. Yes, I will stop, but after just a little bit more… just a little bit more.

I take a deep breath and finish my cocktail. I don't answer my friend. But she has already realized that her message has hit home. For the first time, I've listened.

I look at my wrist again, the one with two stubborn screws that still refuse to move, and I know I screwed up. Literally. Now I have to find my way out of this.

Yes, I will go back to polo. After all, even my cousin, the orthopedic surgeon, says that in order to heal I have to go back to what caused the mess in the first place. I need to find the screwdriver for these screws. I'll go back to polo. But it will have to be in a different way.

The Battle of the Twins

SEPTEMBER

After ten weeks, I'm back at Club Posh again. I've come to fetch my car, my cute blue-and-white Mini that I bought specifically for polo and that was left at the side of the polo field that day when I fell. Everything inside is just as it was that day: my half-drunk protein shake; my helmet, muddy from the fall; my mallets; the shoes I wore before I changed into my polo boots.

A quick stop at the grooms' toilets outside the clubhouse, the place where I used to change when I started with polo, and more memories come flooding back. I am back where it all began, my first polo club, the club where I learned to love polo, the club where I broke my arms.

"Roxy! What are you doing here?" In front of the familiar toilets, I meet a familiar face. This girl plays at Club Real though, not here.

I tell her I'm here to fetch my car, finally, as after ten weeks I can drive again. She tells me she's here to play a game.

"We're playing in the semifinal of the four-goal trophy this weekend. We're starting on ground four in thirty minutes. Cholo is here too!"

I follow her to ground four. A team from Club Real are preparing for the game with two Argentine pros, and Cholo is one of them.

"I'll cheer for you," I say, conscious that on the other side the Club Posh team are getting ready too. Not only does the owner of Club Posh play on that team, but the guy who introduced me to polo, Ziggy's dad, is playing with them as well.

My twins are going into battle with one another. As the two teams line up for the throw-in, I can't help but think that fate is playing games with me: of all the days it had to be this one, when I came back to fetch my car. Of all the people I could meet in front of a toilet, it had to be *this* girl, who had to tell me about *this* game. One way or the other, I was here because fate had decided I must witness my twins playing against each other.

Club Real score a few goals in quick succession. They play well together, and the short Spanish phrases they throw at each other on the field work well to bind their game. Club Posh appear to be surprised, and their game becomes weaker. Club Real carry on with a well-balanced team of two girls and two guys in close coordination. They score more goals.

I walk towards the pony lines at the end of the first chukka, knowing this is where the Club Real team will come to change their horses. I want to congratulate them, to tell them they've been amazing. They come riding their tired ponies in a slow-rising canter. I hurry along, hoping for a moment to talk to them. They only have a few minutes to change horses but I want to tell them "well done."

And as I do, for a moment, I forget. I forget how it feels to be a player, back from a chukka, your mind still replaying the last ride-off, the last shot to the goal. I forget how it is when you realize you have only a few moments to breathe before you need to be back there on another horse, only a few moments before you need to erase the memory of the last hit, of the elbow in your belly from the nasty guy who rode you off… only a few minutes to put all that behind you and go back there and play your best for a new chukka. I forget that they can't really hear me, down here congratulating them. Their eyes are locked on a faraway point back on the field as they change their horses. They are in another dimension; they are still there on the field, in that game, and only they know how that truly feels.

For a moment, I forget all this, and I become just like all the other people who don't play this sport but only watch. And only watching, you cannot really imagine how it feels, what the players have gone through and what they are going back to. I forget that congratulations don't really mean anything when you know you need to go back there and fight for another three chukkas. After ten weeks out of the saddle, I forget what it is to be a player, and I become just a spectator.

They don't answer. They are still far away. Their bodies are going through the automatic routine for the between-chukka time: jump off one horse and onto another, pick up a different-sized mallet, grab a few sips from a water bottle, adjust their goggles, check if the stirrups are right. Then, with a quick look at their teammates and not a word, they are off again.

The rest of the chukkas follow. Club Real are clearly winning. The score is six to one in the last chukka, and I know that no force in the world is going to reverse that.

I sit down on the grass by the safety line in the middle of the field, and Ziggy, the fateful dog who triggered my polo passion, comes and sits with me. He watches his dad playing on the field, getting defeated by Club Real.

I sit with Ziggy and watch the game. I don't know if my wrist will regain its full range of motion. I don't know how I will feel when I'm back on a horse. I don't even know if I'll ever be back on a horse, if I'll ever play polo again. But it doesn't matter: I'm on a polo field, sitting next to a dog, watching my twins battle on the field. And I know that no matter who wins this game, today both of my twins will go. I will only play at one club next season.

In the last chukka, the game appears to be suddenly changing. Club Real slow down. Club Posh pick up, and their riders manage to break away from the players who have been marking them mercilessly. They score, and then they score again. It's now six to three. For a second I think that maybe they will manage to reverse the score completely, but, no, the bell rings the end of the game. Club Real have won by six to three over Club Posh.

Later that night we celebrate the end of the season. I'd had a celebration with Club Posh a couple of nights before at a fancy London nightclub. This time I'm celebrating with Club Real at a Gaucho restaurant in central London.

"Tell me, what happened in the last chukka? Did you let them score?" I ask Cholo after I congratulate him on an amazing game.

His eyes are steady, just as I remember them from the polo field. The same serious gaze with a hint of kindness.

"Of course." He smiles vaguely. "Of course we did. We were winning the game anyway. No need to humiliate them. Let them score a few goals and enjoy it."

I thought so. The change in the last chukka was too obvious.

"How did you guys coordinate this? Did you talk among yourselves when you decided to let them score a few goals?"

He's now smiling fully as he so seldom does.

"Of course not. We don't need to. We just know. We know when it's OK to let them score and when we need to pick up the game again. It was no harm if they scored, so we just slowed down."

I can't help but wonder whether Club Posh would have done the same for them.

Later that evening, it's time to say good-bye. Cholo travels back to Argentina tomorrow. The polo season there is starting just as it finishes here.

"*Hermano, no te mueres!* Brother, do not die!" I hear someone saying good-bye to Cholo.

Once upon a time, I would have thought this was an exaggeration. But now, I know better. People die playing this sport. But for the group of players, grooms, and professionals gathered that evening sharing a meal at the Gaucho restaurant in central London, this was just a distant thought and accepted as part of life.

More important thoughts were on our minds. The season we'd had, the games we'd played, the horses we'd ridden, the friendships we'd formed. The lessons we'd learned. And one way or another, polo seemed to have had one for each of us.

Adios, amigo. Hope to see you back safely next season.

I'll Get You Back on a Horse

OCTOBER

"Rosanna, listen to me. You need to get back on a horse. If in two weeks you don't show up at my farm so that I can get you back on a horse, I'll come fetch you from London."

I tell him that my left wrist isn't yet healed. That my right shoulder is barely OK. The Old Man doesn't want to hear anything, though. No excuses.

"It's all in the head. You need to get back on a horse. You need to get over the fall. You don't need to play just yet, but you need to be back on a horse. Soon."

Eleven weeks after my fall, I drive towards his farm one sunny October morning after the end of the polo season. I don't feel ready, but I know I will never really feel ready. So I decided not to wait for him to fetch me from London as he threatened. I decided to just show up.

The Old Man's farm is exactly as I left it, almost three months ago when I last rode here. Although Cholo has already gone back to Argentina, the *petiseros* are here for another week. They say *hola* with a smile.

I feel nervous as I wait for my horse to be saddled. I am going to ride on the polo field with the Old Man. When I met him at the polo game two weeks after I broke my arms, he had promised to get me back on a horse. And today he will keep his promise.

I thought a lot about how I would feel when I rode a horse again. During these past eleven weeks when I could only dream of horses, I imagined the moment in detail. The glamour, the thrill, the pictures I would take. I imagined it would happen somewhere in Argentina and that I would ride straight into a game, preferably with Cholo shouting "go to the goal" at me across the field as he so often did. I imagined the hot sun on my face and the movement of the horse under me, ready to go.

None of these things are happening today. They bring out a very stable and calm horse I've never been on before. "You only walk today," the Old Man says. "That's why you have this horse. We never play him: he's too lazy."

I want to protest, to tell him that my dream of getting back on a horse was different, to tell him that although my left wrist is still in a splint on top of my polo glove, I feel I can do it: gallop again, maybe even stick and ball.

But his eyes are tough. He doesn't smile.

"No way. Only walk today. You must learn to be patient. This is going to take a long time."

But… all the words slowly fade in my throat. This is a different type of polo.

"You need to get back to this gradually," the Old Man carries on as we walk on the polo field. "Today, it's for your mind. So you remember how it feels to be back on a horse. Then, next time you come, you'll go for a hack. This is all you need to do this winter. And then, when the spring comes, you'll start to stick and ball again."

Spring is a long time away. I cannot bear to think I will need to wait that long. Maybe if I go to Argentina, Cholo will get me playing sooner.

"And no Argentina this winter." The Old Man has read my thoughts. "It's too early. Only this. Walk, then trot, then canter. Go for a hack to the pub in the next village, have a drink there, and come back."

I so badly want to run. At least one gallop across the field, just to get that adrenaline shot my body craves so badly.

"No run today." He's merciless. "Too dangerous. You haven't been on a horse for so long, and you may fall again. And even if you don't fall, even if you run and everything is fine, why risk it? Why be impatient? You're going to achieve nothing."

And there and then, after twenty minutes of walking around on a polo field with the Old Man next to me, I suddenly get it. This is going to be my new polo. I'm on an adrenaline detox program and somehow, without any explanation, he knows this is exactly what I need right now.

No, it will not be as I imagined. There will be no glamour, no thrill, no adrenaline kick in the blood: not for a good while at least. No sun in Argentina, no fun galloping on the beach. That will come too, but it will be another time, and maybe another story. For now, I make peace with this new version of reality as it unfolds, here on the field, still green despite the end of the polo season, with the Old Man walking his horse beside me and talking about his own polo injuries and how long it took him to recover from them.

It's just the two of us on the field, just as it was at the beginning of the summer, that day with gray skies when I had my first training session with him. He pushed me hard that day, far out of my comfort zone, and I remember how badly I clung to the saddle, out of breath and out of strength. Now he pushes me again, but the other way. He pushes me out of my adrenaline addiction and on to another type of polo.

There will be many more days like this. The walk will move to trot, then canter; the half swing will become a full swing; my arm will hurt, but I will try again; my wrist will move; another operation might follow and my screws might be taken out. There will be many more days like this, and I will live them as they come. In my heart I know he's right. By next spring I'll be ready to play again. And by then, hopefully, my addiction will be tamed, and my passion will survive.

<h1 style="text-align:center">Forty Polo Balls</h1>

NOVEMBER

"*Que lo cumples feliz!* Happy birthday to you!" they all sing around the big table in the living room, and I watch them one by one. I watch them silently, trying to hold back my tears.

Gabriela to my right, her face covered by her shoulder-length, curly blond hair, carefully deposits on the table a dark chocolate cake displaying an impressive horse's head and a small candle. I guess it would have been impossible to fit forty candles on the cake, not without damaging the horse's head decoration, and if you ask me, I'd rather have the horse's head.

I had no idea such things existed. Like chocolate horse's head birthday cakes. But everything is possible in Argentina. These people turn the impossible into the possible, and they don't even think twice about it.

It was my fortieth birthday, and for the past few months I'd had quite a hard time getting used to the idea I was going to face such a milestone birthday still single and without polo, as I was still busy regaining the use of my arms.

Then Gabriela came to visit me in London, on her way back to Argentina, and, upon hearing all about my anguish, she came up with a very straightforward solution.

"Come spend your birthday at the farm, she said matter of factly as if she were talking about going to the pub down the road. "And don't you worry, darling, we'll turn you forty, and you're going to be just fine!"

She told me she would organize a girls' party where she, Rosario, and two other girlfriends, all just slightly older than me, would take good care of me and show me that there was indeed life after forty.

It was too good an offer to refuse. I went to work the next day and spoke to my boss. I had started working again, and had just accepted a new six-month contract. I still couldn't play polo, but my arms had recovered enough to be able to lead a normal life, so I couldn't hide away from work any longer.

My boss thought I was crazy to ask for three days off to go all the way to Argentina. Actually, it would be a five-day trip, counting the weekend as well, I told him. I also told him that I would be turning forty, that I was single and desperately looking, and that all these facts pointed to one obvious conclusion: it was a lot safer for him to give me three days off than have to deal with me in the office on the day of such a troublesome birthday.

He agreed. He was a smart guy, my boss, and he knew how this fortieth-birthday thing was for women. So I bought myself an airline ticket and was picked up at the airport by Gabriela, driving Patricio's minivan with one hand and juggling a bottle of beer with the other.

"Girl, are you crazy? What about the no drink and drive rules?"

"Relax, darling, you are in Argentina now!" she said as she took another sip from the bottle.

So I relaxed. She took me to the farm, straight to a lovely dinner with all the family, and then she produced this surprise chocolate cake as everybody else stood up and started singing.

My birthday is tomorrow, I want to say, but then I say nothing. Maybe this is how they do things in Argentina, a bit differently. So I just try hard to hold back my tears as I watch them all singing: Patricio and Gabriela; their son, a smiley five-year-old; Patricio's father, the owner of the farm and the patriarch of the family, seated at the top of the table; Patricio's sister; her husband and three kids. And even Rosario, who has shown up by surprise just in time for the dinner.

The singing comes to an end, and I take a big breath ready to blow out the candle.

"Remember to make a wish!" someone says, I'm not sure who.

May this year finally bring me a boyfriend, I think as I blow out my fortieth-birthday candle. It would be the perfect gift. If I'm really honest with myself, I want a boyfriend even more than I want to get back to playing polo.

But the Universe decides I'm not yet done with playing polo. Just as I finish blowing out the candle, Gabriela produces another of her surprises: a straw bag filled with forty polo balls. "Polo addict" she has written on the bag in big letters with white paint. So that I remember.

I laugh at the label and push it to a very hidden corner of my mind. I pick up the bulky bag and hold it in my arms for a while, close to my heart: forty polo balls to mark my fortieth birthday.

"Now you have to score a goal with each of them!" Patricio says, and they all laugh. "And you have a good reason to come back here, once your arms are strong enough to hold a mallet," he adds.

This birthday is starting out well, I think. Tomorrow we'll go to Buenos Aires for a girls' party and a big night out, but I already know that it's today, the evening before my birthday, that I will always remember for my fortieth.

There's no way I can carry this heavy bag back to London with me, so I take just one ball, one small white hard plastic polo ball, and ask them each to write something on it.

"Love" is the first thing that catches my eye as the ball comes back to me. Repeated over and over again, in each of their messages.

Last year I spent Christmas and New Year's Eve with them. This year, it's my birthday. I'm not sure what binds me to these people, but I'm sure of one thing: There will be many more occasions to be with them in the future.

Back in the Saddle

It's been a long winter. I focused on recovery. My shoulder healed. My wrist not fully, but it's more functional now. I had intensive physiotherapy for three months. Then, for another three months, I went to the gym, gaining strength and lifting weights. On the weekends, I rode horses. I went skiing and realized how much the fall was still preying on my mind every time I went fast. I came back. More gym, more riding. Then, I went skiing again. And all of a sudden, the memory of the fall was no longer there.

Then spring arrived, and just like the Old Man predicted, I felt ready to play again.

And one morning I got back on a horse, my stomach bubbling with excitement, my heart pounding with fear, the familiar smell of leather and horse sweat in my nose, and my body rocking to the rhythm of the horse's hooves. First walk, then trot, then canter. I picked up speed quickly, and soon I found myself in a flat gallop across the polo field.

"Let go!" The voice of my coach flashes though my mind, and I relax my wrist and give the mare rein. Too much control gets in the way of a horse that runs flat out; I learned that long ago. I trust that she will go, and she trusts that I will guide her. She is relaxed; I can feel her long, powerful body stretching under me with every stride. But, at the same time, she is tense too, as one is when running at full speed. I feel good in the saddle, my body moving along to replicate her moves. And yet I feel the panic as well. That inexplicable blend of panic and excitement that fuels the adrenaline rush.

I lift slightly from the saddle so she can breathe easier, tilt my upper body a little bit forward, and move my feet back to keep my balance. I arch my back, straighten my shoulders, and now my heart opens fully and beams forward, connected to the world, to the wind, and to the horse beneath me. From that place in between two worlds, not really seated and not really raised up in the saddle either, I feel the weightless shape of my own body and the powerful energy of the animal beneath me. For a moment, I worry about losing this subtle balance, and I wonder how much it will hurt this time if I fall again. I let the thought come, and then I let it go, and the memory of the fall and of the pain goes away with it. I am back where I belong: once again flying on the back of a horse.

I guide my horse towards the ball simply by looking at it. It feels like magic, but one of my coaches once explained to me that by looking at the ball, I tilt my head slightly in that direction, which changes the weight on the back of the horse, and this is how she knows where to go. I don't care if it's true or not; I just know that I am so connected to this animal that she goes flat out wherever I look, as if she is reading my thoughts.

"Push with your knee into the saddle!" he shouts from somewhere behind me, and then the last piece of the puzzle finally falls into place.

My body lines up from my left heel to my knee, pushed into the saddle, then up through my twisted hip straight across my abdomen and further up into my right arm, which now opens up in a familiar pendulum-swing pose. I hear the familiar *click* sound of a ball well hit, and I know, even before I lift my eyes from where they have been locked, straight above the ball. I already know it's been a good hit, and it will go far.

"*Buena!*" shouts Patricio from his horse. A good one.

After nine months out of the saddle, I am finally hitting a good shot again.

I'm in Spain training with Patricio in a polo club outside Barcelona where he plays professionally. When I visited them last November, he told me he would be here in March and invited me to come train with him for a few days. "I'll get you back on a horse," he promised. Just like the Old Man did.

So I went. I met them both, Patricio and Gabriela, and we had a bottle of red wine and laughed at the memory of my forty polo balls left behind in Argentina. They asked if my birthday wish to finally meet Mr. Right had materialized, and I told them it hadn't. I'd met a few potential Mr. Rights, the most important of whom was my physiotherapist, a tall, broad-shouldered, dark-haired biker, who tortured my wrist twice a week in the hope of making it move while I tried to chat him up. Eventually, unimpressed by my chat-up attempts, he decided there was nothing else he could do for my wrist, and he sent me back to my doctor, the one who operated on me. The doctor checked again and confirmed the recommendation of both my cousin, the orthopedic surgeon, and my physio: I needed additional surgery.

It wasn't urgent, he said. I could come in whenever I wanted, but I had to bear in mind that I would need extensive rehabilitation afterwards, and I wouldn't be able to play polo for a while, two maybe three months after surgery.

I decided to forget about it. The polo season was about to start in England. And I wasn't going to lose this one, not after losing half of the previous season immobilized in bed. Not again. My wrist was good enough to hold the reins of a horse, so I told my doctor that I would have surgery at the end of the season, in October. And then I erased the word surgery from my mind.

I went to Spain instead, to train with Patricio, and I called the Old Man to tell him I was planning to have a full season this year. Both were enthusiastic and happy for me. My return to polo was becoming a reality.

After a long-overdue catch-up with news of my love life and upcoming surgery, Patricio suggested I get back on a horse. There's nothing a good session of polo can't take care of, he said.

And this is where it all fell into place. Like the fall had never happened, and all these months of silent suffering had never been. In a few seconds, my body found its balance again, and my mallet found the ball. And I forgot about surgery, nonexistent boyfriends, and fear of other falls.

Thoughtless, weightless, effortless… I let myself fly.

And then, later, after the stick-and-ball session, I ask Patricio to show me how to do that cool move of his, when he jumps from one horse to the other in between chukkas. He agrees, and we try at a slow pace with the horses nicely tied one next to the other. I'm supposed to put one foot on top of the saddle, lift the other from the stirrup, stretch it across the second horse, and in one go push myself out of the first saddle and into the second one.

I do everything just as he explains, but something doesn't go according to plan. I find myself sliding in between the horses and, with one desperate move, I heave myself across the saddle of the second horse, just like a sack of potatoes.

Gabriela laughs and starts taking pictures. This girl is always ready to take pictures. I laugh too, slightly embarrassed by the disastrous end to my professional polo move while Patricio remarks in a patient voice, "There's a time for everything. Maybe you're moving a little bit too fast."

And with this, I get it. I might be back to polo, but I'm still a long way from being a real polo player. But I have a full season ahead of me to make sure I'll become one.

Surprise on a Polo Field

APRIL

"Wait, Rosanna! Wait for me here!" says the Old Man with a mysterious smile.

I don't really want to wait. The polo season has officially started, and I'm back at his club, freshly returned from my training with Patricio in Spain. All I want is to get on a horse and get going.

But the Old Man has another plan.

"You wait for me here," he repeats firmly. "I have something for you."

So I wait because one can't argue with the Old Man. He's got that way of giving orders in a somewhat laid-back manner but at the same time crystal clear. He is accustomed to being obeyed on a polo field, and even if we're only at the edge of one now, his words still command attention.

I'm fully dressed for my stick-and-ball lesson. Helmet, boots, gloves, the full kit. I've even got my Oakley glasses, though they're not really required when stick and balling. I've been dreaming of this day ever since last year when, at the end of the season in

October, he put me back on a horse for a walk across the polo field and told me I would be ready to play in the spring. Well, spring is here, and I *am* ready.

I came to the club full of hope that I would find Cholo and the rest of the familiar faces, but the first surprise was that Cholo was gone, still in Argentina, busy with other polo jobs, and he would not return this season. In his place, a very young guy introduced himself as Jonny. He would be the new professional player, the Old Man told me. I eyed him suspiciously. He must have been in his early twenties. Not that Cholo was much older, but he had a way of carrying himself with a quiet self-confidence and mysterious smile, which, coupled with the very few words he said, gave him an air of undisputable authority. Jonny, on the other hand, was smiling all the time and very talkative. He would come to stick and ball with me, the Old Man had told me before he disappeared.

I wait on the side of the polo field, swallowing my disappointment at Cholo's absence and my irritation at the Old Man's delays. I can't do much about either and, besides, polo is all about living in the present.

"Surprise!" the Old Man suddenly exclaims from somewhere behind my back.

I turn around and see his wide smile, ear to ear. In his hands are the reins of a dark, chocolate-colored horse that watches me with friendly, big brown eyes.

"What?" I ask, still grumpy.

"*Sorpresa!*" he repeats, in Spanish this time. Then he points to the horse behind him. "This is Sorpresa. Surprise. A surprise for you. She will be one of your horses for the season."

My horse. He means my leased horse, since I have no intention of buying one. Not yet, at least. But he had mentioned to me he would give me a couple of horses on lease for the full duration of the season so I could get accustomed to how it feels to ride and play the same horses. And care for them. Like a true player would.

Sorpresa doesn't seem phased by the loud introduction; she just stretches her neck to be patted as I approach her. She is already saddled, a comfortable, large suede saddle, the kind of saddle I like. Professional players prefer the smooth leather saddles where they can slide easily from one movement to another. But for me, a suede saddle with a much firmer grip would do.

"She is an easy horse, a very gentle one, but she is fast too," the Old Man continues. "She is the perfect horse for you. A darling. I've had her in mind for you for some time. She will help you get back into the game, you'll see."

I get into the saddle, and I notice that, indeed, Sorpresa has a very comfy stride. Horses feel different when you ride them; some have very shaky strides and some move up and down a lot more; some have short strides and some longer.

But Sorpresa is just perfect, I decide after a few rounds of warm-up canter around the polo field with Jonny at my side.

"Shall we hit some balls, Roxana?" Jonny says, and I nod my head, surprised he doesn't call me Rosanna as the Old Man, Cholo, and all Argentines do, or Roxy like my other friends. On the contrary, Jonny makes a point of pronouncing the *x* in my name perfectly clearly.

I hit some balls, and I then take another look at him as he rides in front of me. On the horse, with his dark polo helmet on, Jonny looks completely transformed. He is no longer a smiley kid trying to make conversation. His moves are certain, his body floating above the saddle in a perfect half seat. The mallet in his hand moves elegantly and hits the balls in a long, straight line every time. He guides his horse seamlessly, with slow and confident moves, and even his voice sounds different as he shouts instructions to me across the field.

"Good shot! Now again. Backhand to me. Hit. Now!" And then: "Too late. I said now. Next time do as I say."

And without further doubts, I decide he is my new Cholo, and I will do as he says.

Thirty minutes later, which is as long as a horse can run on the stick-and-ball field, I return to the stables, jump off my Sorpresa, and look around to check where the Old Man might be. He's nowhere to be seen. Instead, I see a chubby teenage boy with a wide smile on his face, just like Jonny's, hurrying towards me, holding the reins of another horse.

"*Para mi?*" I ask him as he approaches. For me?

"*Si.*" He nods, holding the horse still so I can mount.

"*Como se llama?*" What's her name? I ask him. I always like to know the names of the horses I'm riding.

"Pedrito!" His smile becomes even wider. He points to himself and repeats "Pedrito. *Soy tu petisero.*"

He is my groom, he says. And his name is Pedrito, something like little Pedro, I guess. He's not that little though; on the contrary, he's quite chubby and well built. I feel a stab of embarrassment that I asked the name of the horse before his own name, but the Spanish language has saved me. *Como se llama* means both what is she called and what are you called if I use the formal form of the verb.

"*Ah, bueno.*" I recover my mistake. "*Encantada.* Nice to meet you. I'm Roxy. And her?" I point clearly to the horse this time.

"*Pampita,*" he says.

I try not to burst out laughing. From my short stay in Argentina I remember Pampita as a famous model and television actress. A half-Brazilian, half-Argentine beauty with long brown hair, big boobs, and a charming smile. At least the horse is the color of her light brown locks.

With all these introductions done, I don't ask anything else. I take my new horse onto the polo field, alone this time. Jonny, who trained with me for the first half-hour, is busy now. He's both a professional player and a groom, and I bet he's got a lot to do.

I feel a bit sad and I'm not sure why. I have two nice horses, Pampita and Sorpresa, who will be mine for the season, the Old Man said, and I know he keeps his word. Cholo is gone, it's true, but his replacement, Jonny, looks like someone who can do the job. And the polo season has started, and I'm really going to enjoy this one, not like last year when things got out of hand.

And yet, a part of me, the one that feels the sadness, tells me that I've just pressed replay on a movie I've already seen.

It's not replay, silly. I try to silence the voice inside. I'm moving forward. I'm playing polo because it's my passion. My love coach told me to get in touch with my passion, right? Well, I've done it.

The silly voice reminds me that it was all about finding Mr. Right, and he was still nowhere in sight.

He will come. I shrug my shoulders and nudge my horse into a warm-up canter.

When the right time comes, he will come. I know he will.

And Finally I Play

MAY

Before we line up for the start of the game, we line up for the team photo. It's the first tournament of the season. The first tournament in my polo life. Last year, I only played friendly chukkas, games where we don't keep the score and, as a result, no one takes them too seriously. But now, all of a sudden, things are different. I am playing a real tournament. With a professional player on the team, with scores and trophies. Now, all of a sudden, things matter. Much more than they ever had.

I ride Sorpresa for the first chukka. She's easier in the mouth than Pampita and has a more comfortable stride. She'll ease me well into the game, I know it. I take her to the center of the field and speak to her in the usual whisper. I tell her we're going to play a tournament and that all will be well. I promise her I'll look after her and keep her safe. And keep myself safe, too, I add, just for good measure, the memory of my fall dancing in front of my eyes for a second. I imagine a white protective cloud engulfing us both, horse and rider, as if we are one being, and I imagine growing roots through my legs and sending them down through her legs, down into the center of the earth. And then I tell her once again: We will be safe, I promise you. Just play with me. She hears me, I know she does.

I line up next to my teammates and as I do I make sure I arch my back, pulling my shoulder backwards. I remember the words of one of my old coaches at Club Posh: "Keep your shoulders back! We polo people are proud people!"

The memory of my former Club Posh evaporates just like the memory of the fall as I watch the other team riding towards the center of the field. I haven't been back to Club Posh since I saw Cholo play in the final game of the last season. I now only play here at Club Real, under the careful supervision of the Old Man. We line up the horses neatly in front of the other team, only a small corridor left between the players. This is where the umpire will throw the ball in and shout *Play*. And then the fun will start.

We line up and wait. There are always a few minutes of waiting, this surreal time just before the umpire throws the ball in, when your body is still relaxed, but you know it will get tense very soon, as soon as the ball leaves the umpire's hand. And the horses know it too. A few minutes when you fill your lungs with air and feel inexplicably but powerfully alive, as if the game that's about to start has suddenly made you conscious of how precious your life is.

Yes, I am alive. And happy. And grateful to have regained the use of my arms enough that I can play this game, my first tournament. I'll remember it forever.

I look at my teammates, one by one. They smile back at me and nod. They, all of them players much better than me, know it's my first tournament. They'll look after me; they'll tell me what to do, I know they will. And then, there's the player with number four, the Old Man. He plays as the professional in our team, and this gives me a lot of confidence. Nothing bad can happen to me on a polo field as long as the Old Man is there with me.

"Rosanna!" He shouts at me from his horse as if answering my unspoken thoughts. "Today you finally play!"

And then a few moments later, the umpire echoes him, throwing the small white plastic ball in between us, two perfectly lined-up teams, and the shout fills my soul, and the adrenaline gets released in one big shot into my veins and into the veins of my horse as well.

Plaaay!

In one sudden move, the stillness of the previous second is gone, and we all fly in different directions. My teammate has the ball. I burst out in a gallop in front of him, positioning myself at a reasonable distance for a potential shot. My other teammate, number two, speeds up laterally, opening up another possible shot for the guy with the ball. Behind me I hear the gallop of a player from the other team; he'll come to mark me, no doubt, and try to stop me receiving the ball. I must have my stick-side free. I suddenly remember the Old Man's advice just as the other player comfortably installs himself to my right. Shit! But there's no time for thinking. I hear the click behind and realize the ball has now been sent forward, but not to me, to number two.

Move! Move on! The game is picking up speed, and I know I have to be ahead in the field. I'm playing as number one.

"Rosanna! Slow down!" Amid the thunderous noise of Sorpresa's hooves running across the field, I hear from far behind the voice of the Old Man.

"Too fast. You go too fa-a-a-st!"

He should be happy I'm going so fast; a flash goes through my mind but I've no time to dwell on it. Polo is a game of the present moment. The ball is coming my way. I can see it. I direct my horse towards it and rise up in half seat preparing to hit.

But the Old Man is right: I must have gone too fast because I cannot slow the horse down enough, and Sorpresa now runs as if she's seen the devil hiding in the bushes around the field, and there's no way of slowing her down. I miss the ball. I miss because I hurry, and my swing is too fast. I know it even before I hear the familiar shout:

"Too fast! I told you to slow down!" I detect a hint of irritation in the Old Man's voice this time. He's accustomed to being obeyed on a polo field.

The ball has now been picked up by the guy who was marking me and sent back with an elegant backhand. I turn my horse in a wide circle, wide enough for her to understand that I mean to go back. She slows down finally, but then I push my hand with the reins forward and lift up in half seat again, and she understands she needs to run faster, the other way now.

"Rosanna! Slow down!"

I've had enough of the Old Man's constant attention. I check my position against the other players and, no, I'm not too far ahead. Why is he watching my speed so obsessively?

"Sloow down! Rosanna-a-a-a! I want to protect you!" He screams the answer to my unspoken question in plain hearing of everyone on the field, and I feel my cheeks blushing, and I'm grateful that there's no one close enough to me to notice.

So now the whole field knows the Old Man is there to protect me. I swallow my irritation and decide to ignore his shouts. There's nothing to be done once the Old Man chooses to fixate his attention on you. You can only hope something more interesting will come along, and he'll let you be for a while.

And something does. Because polo is like that; you can't dwell on what happened a moment ago. The Old Man is now busy trying to take the ball from the inexperienced number one player of the other team and, sure enough, it only takes him a moment to do so.

"Rosanna!" He screams as he slowly turns the ball in canter.

I brace up for the irritating slow-down instruction again, but none comes, not this time.

"Go forward. Go! Go, Rosanna! I'm going to send the ball to you! Faster!"

I let out a sigh as I lift up again in the stirrups and turn Sorpresa around. At last we are over the babysitting phase.

The chukkas go on one after the other in a blur.

I feel the connection to the horse viscerally as if she's part of my body, and I know she feels me as if I'm inside her head. And I am connected to my teammates too. Like an invisible line that binds us, one body with four shapes, I know where they are on the field and where they're going. I know what they're thinking about; I anticipate their hits and place myself correctly to receive the ball. I know when they have a better shot, and I leave the ball to them whether they ask for it or not. I feel when they are struggling, and I move to help them, against an adversary. I know how they feel because I feel it too. We are alive. We are connected. And there is no way to explain it and no comparison to it. We are high. We are polo high.

Then at some point during the last chukka, I hear a loud scream from the other side of the field. I hurry over with my horse and I see the professional player from the other team, a big, strong Argentine, crunched in the saddle holding his mallet arm towards his chest.

He cries out in pain and jumps down from the saddle, still holding his right arm to his chest. He's been hit. A hook most likely. The whistle blows, the game stops. We gather around him, all of us still in the saddle. Jonny, who also plays on the other team, gets off his horse and goes to comfort the injured player. He's stopped screaming, but we're not quite sure if he can play again.

I feel tears welling up as I hear his screams. But there's nothing we can do. There's no point in dismounting and gathering around him to find out what happened while the horses run wild everywhere. So we just stay there, mounted on our horses, next to the umpire, looking at the first-aid car that drives slowly onto the field.

Then it looks like he'll be OK. He can still move his fingers, and this means it's likely there's nothing broken. On his arm I can see deep blue marks where the cane of another player's mallet hit him instead of the ball.

A few minutes later, his arm frozen with a spray and the pain taken away for the time being, he decides to get back into the saddle for the last three minutes of the game. Jonny helps him mount his horse. His right arm grabs the mallet with a sudden determination.

"*Vamos*," he yells. "*Dale, vamos.*"

He *will* play. He will not leave his teammates to finish the game with only three players, because there is no one who can substitute for him.

We wait for the first-aid car to leave the field, then line up again, with the mallets down this time. There's another throw-in; there always is after the umpire blows the whistle for injury and, all of a sudden, the accident is erased from our minds because the ball is back on the field again, and we can't think of anything else but the ball.

We have three minutes to go, and that's a lot of time. Before polo I thought three minutes went by in the blink of an eye, but I now know better. Today three minutes is all we need to win the game, the other team now weakened by an injured player.

We manage to score the winning goal just before the umpire blows the end of the game and, of course, it is the Old Man who scores it. He's full of surprises, the Old Man. He usually plays in a laid-back manner and lets us, the rest of the team, struggle and score. But every now and then, when it truly matters, he mysteriously gets activated, and then there's action on the field. Just like now when he recovered the ball from number one of the opposite team, turned it around with a few quick clicks, and then sent it straight between the goalposts with one long, powerful shot.

We won! The handshake at the end of the game follows, and I feel like I'm floating somewhere high above the ground, the horse and my teammates with faces drenched in sweat. We ride our horses in circles, remembering to shake hands with everyone on our team, with the umpire, and with the players of the other team as well.

"Thank you, it was a great game!" is all we say. And they, the guys who lost, thank us too.

Then I jump off my horse and hand the reins to Pedrito, who hands me in exchange my bottle of water that he has been carefully guarding. He's a good groom, Pedrito, always attentive to what I need.

I'm happy we won, but the bitter taste in my mouth is still there, just slightly hidden by the thrill of winning my first tournament game. I can't stop thinking of the player who got hurt and his swollen arm. And his work as a groom is only just starting now: the horses needs to be unsaddled, bathed, and taken to the fields; the tack need to be cleaned, gathered from the fields, put back into the tack room… and then, towards the end of the day, the riding boots of the clients need to be polished as well. All this is part of a groom's work, while we, the members of the club, sit down, debate the highs and the lows of the game with a drink in our hands, and enjoy a well-deserved barbecue.

We take another team photo just before we sit down to have our lunch. It's a trophy-holding photo, all four players of our team with the small cup we've been fighting for. Then we take a photo with the other team as well. The injured guy comes running from the pony lines, takes his groom's T-shirt off, and puts his player's T-shirt on. He smiles with the rest of us for the photo. Then he takes the sweaty player's shirt off again and reverts back to being a groom. His hand is now carefully covered in a neat white bandage. I suspect the Old Man must be the one who did it.

Jonny has gone to see to his grooming duties too. Far off, towards the back of the pony lines, I see Pedrito finish washing Pampita, the horse I played in the last chukka, and getting ready to release both Sorpresa and her into the field. There's a lot of work behind the scenes here, but in polo this isn't usually the job of a player.

The Old Man pours himself a cup of *mate*, content that the tournament went well and no one was injured, at least not seriously. The players sit at the picnic tables and fill their plates with delicious potato salad, veggies, and a generous serving of grilled lamb. Four lambs have been slowly roasting on a campfire ever since morning.

I add some Fanta to the rest of the wine in my glass, trying to recreate a taste of Sangria since there's no Campari orange here, and I sit down next to my teammates contemplating my dirty white jeans.

I'll have to remember to bring another pair to change into after the game, I think as I slowly sip my drink. I'll make sure I remember for the next game.

In polo, there's always a next game to think about.

What Happens on the Field Stays on the Field

JUNE

Tonny has become a friend. I'm not even sure when this happened, but I realize it one day in the middle of the summer as I arrive at the Old Man's farm, ready for my stick-and-ball training.

I'm now coming to stick and ball two or three times a week. I finished the work project that kept me going over the winter and didn't look for another one. I justified it by saying this is my year of polo, when I'll make up for the season I lost last year. And polo is like this. It requires time.

And money, my rational self adds.

Yes, and money too, I reply.

And where are you going to get all this money if you don't work? she continues the questioning.

I'll work later when the season is over.

Then you need to have the second surgery on your hand, remember?

Yes, I remember. I'll do it afterwards! My rational self is very stubborn sometimes, and I'm quick to lose patience with her.

This will take you to the end of the year. And how much longer do you think you can go on spending money like this on polo? she continues, unimpressed.

Shut up, you bitch. You don't understand.

And, moreover, you're still single. So much for your brilliant plan to meet the man of your dreams! She's ironic now, which is the worst tone of all.

I'm trying hard to ignore her. I close my eyes and push these thoughts as far away as possible, and when I open them again Jonny is in front of me holding two horses by the reins. One for him and my Sorpresa for me. And suddenly there are no more thoughts as I mount my horse and ride leisurely towards the stick-and-ball field.

Jonny and I talk about everything when we train. We talk as we take the horses to the field, we talk as we canter to warm them up, and we even talk between the shots or when we slow down and take a walk, giving the horses time to breathe.

He tells me about the girls he likes back in Argentina—quite a few of them—and I tell him about the perfect man I'm hoping to meet. One day. Then we talk about life in England, about life in Argentina, about horses, polo, mallets and games. And then we come back to dating. I guess this is the most interesting subject of all, for both of us.

"I cannot understand why you're single, really," he says as he sends the ball far towards the end of the field in one long, straight line. I wish I could hit like this.

"I don't either!" I shrug my shoulders as I nudge my horse into a canter towards the ball. I'm going to do a backhand, I decide.

Jonny stays behind me. He's probably guessed I'm going to send the ball back to him.

"Now! Hit!" I hear the command from behind and I obey the very second I hear it.

It was the right timing; the ball goes back in a nice line and lands close to Jonny's horse.

"*Buena!*" he shouts. And then, "Have you looked around enough here? There are many nice guys who come and play at this club."

Yes, I have looked hard enough and, yes, there are a lot of nice guys who play polo here. Some of them have steady girlfriends. Others have a string of would-be girlfriends coming to cheer for them. One of them in particular brings a different girlfriend to every game. We all get really confused trying to make conversation with the girls he brings, because we can't remember if we've met them before, and we don't want to say something wrong that would make them realize they are not the only one to accompany their man to a polo game.

It's like this for men in polo: they have no shortage of admirers. But it's quite a different story for girls in polo. For a start, because you don't want to date someone you play with. If things go sour, you're still going to play at the same club and then you have to put up with the long string of female admirers your ex-boyfriend will bring along, game after game for eternity. Not a pretty sight. The only alternative would be to change polo clubs, but it's not worth losing your club over a romance gone bad. So, it's a lose-lose situation. Of course, there's the happy ending where you play polo and the love of your life plays polo at the same club too. Forever. But I haven't seen that happen. If couples play polo together and they don't break up, one of them, usually the woman, gives up polo after a while. The standard excuse is pregnancy and child-rearing. I'm not sure this is the real reason, or whether the field is simply not big enough for two people to be in love and play polo together. Maybe each could play at a different club. Which could work technically, but polo is such a time-intensive game that you would end up spending all your time on separate polo fields. Hardly an option.

A couple of girls who play here have boyfriends who don't play polo. Now that would be a possibility. Only they met those boyfriends before they started to play polo and had a lot of time for socializing. One way or the other, the painful truth about love and polo slowly made its way into my mind: Guys who play polo are in demand by the opposite sex. Girls who play polo are not.

Ah, and there's one more avenue available to women in polo, a very popular one. Falling in love with the professional polo player, usually the one you train or play with. I have heard so many stories involving this particular scenario that I make sure to stay well clear of it. It never really works.

So I tell Jonny that, yes, I have had a good look around the club, but it doesn't look like my Mr. Right plays polo there.

"Then you have to meet him somewhere else!" he concludes as we slow down the horses for a breathing break. "How often do you go out?"

Not very often, that's the problem. I'm too busy playing polo. Friday and Saturday nights I don't usually go out because we have tournament games the following mornings, and I want to be fresh and ready. Then, Sunday night I'm usually too tired from the weekend games so I just drive home from the polo field and go straight to bed. During the week… well, I could go out during the week, but two nights we play practice games, and I don't want to miss those, and then I'm not even sure how this whole business of going out works anymore because I've been out of the non-polo social scene for a while. Even my friends outside polo got used to my constant excuses, so I've gradually been left out.

"Yes, I have to go out more. But even when I do go out, men seem not to notice me. I don't know what's wrong with me!" I sigh.

"There's nothing wrong with you." Jonny turns his head to look me straight in the eyes. His eyes are deep and brown and look sincere.

"Believe me. You are a beautiful woman."

That counts as a compliment from someone half my age. I smile.

"Come on, I've just turned forty! I'm officially an old lady now. Who will ever want to date me?"

"I know a bunch of people who would love to date you!" He smiles encouragingly.

"Where?" My heart races with hope.

"In Argentina. We appreciate a beautiful woman when we see one. Come to Argentina. You will not be single for long, I promise you," he says with a definite certainty in his voice.

Argentina seems a long way away, and I've already been there and nothing happened. I tell this to Jonny.

"You haven't looked in the right places. Did you live with the Argentines?" he asks.

"Hmm, not really. I lived mostly in polo estancias, played polo with foreigners, and then I stayed with a local family, they are very lovely!"

"Yes, but you're not going to meet your guy playing polo with foreigners or staying with an Argentine family," he replies.

"But how, Jonny?" I shrug my shoulders again, discouraged.

"Come live like an Argentine, go out in Buenos Aires. *Sola*. Alone. You'll see what happens!" He seems very certain of the outcome.

"You think so?" I'm half convinced.

"I know so," he replies. "You will see. Trust me. We Argentine men, we really appreciate beautiful women!"

The horses have had enough of a rest, so we nudge them into a canter again. We ride in circles, and Jonny teaches me how to turn the ball with small hits. One, two, three, four, the clicks of the mallet on the ball sound like a rhythmic melody as he takes the ball in a complete circle.

"Now you go!" He passes the ball over to me.

I rise in my stirrups and try to copy his posture, bent over to my right, my head sticking out above the ball, my left knee twisted and pushed into the saddle. I get the horse into a slow canter. *Click, click, click…* And I lose it.

"Again!" shouts Jonny, unimpressed. "We stay here until you reach twenty."

This is going to be a hell of a long day, I think as I turn my horse around and start again: one, two three, four…

"It's impossible. Maybe I can try again next time!" I try to find a way out.

"Come on!" he says, unimpressed. "Nothing is impossible! Not twenty hits in a row, and not even finding a boyfriend! All you need to do is believe that you can. Now try again."

It takes a while, but I finally manage to still my mind enough to reach twenty. I'm very pleased with my achievement. The alternative would have been to stay there forever, I'm sure. Jonny means what he says.

With the stick-and-ball session finished, we walk slowly towards the stables, and Jonny explains in detail once again the philosophy of the perfect small hit. I'm only half-listening. My mind goes back and forth between two equally satisfying thoughts. The first one is that I've managed to score twenty small hits in a row. That's more than I ever dreamed of. Jonny is right, all I need to do is believe that I can. And the second thought is that maybe Jonny is right about something else too.

Maybe I should go back to Argentina.

Like It's Never Been

JULY

Pedrito displays a very mischievous smile as he brings me the horse all tacked up and ready for the game. I know that smile well, it means he's up to something. I've come to know Pedrito very well in the three months that he's been my groom. He understands me almost without words. Where's my horse? My bottle of water? Stirrups are too long, then too short. Eventually he puts a mark on the leather straps of the stirrups at the perfect length for me. So that he remembers. "Rosanna's mark," he says proudly as he shows me the sign. "The saddle will always be perfect for you."

My boots are always perfectly polished too, and my horse perfectly tacked. Or at least this is how we started. Then something got into me, I'm not sure what, and I told him I wanted to learn to tack a horse myself. He seemed puzzled—why would I want to do this? Players don't normally take an interest in tacking and untacking a polo horse; this is the groom's job. And he does it quite well.

I assured him that it wasn't because I didn't trust him but

because I really wanted to learn how to do it. He agreed to teach me. And we had a few sessions in the stables where I learned all the moves one by one under his careful supervision. Only I was much slower—by the time I managed to put a bandage on one of the horse's legs, for instance, he had the other three done. Eventually I got tired of these lessons and gave up. I told him I'd learned enough. But ever since, he got into the habit of playing little tricks with me. So I started noticing that the previously perfectly tacked horses now started to have bits of tack missing or misplaced. I spotted them every time before I got into the saddle, and this usually brought a big smile to his face.

"Well done, Rosanna!" he congratulated me. "Well spotted. I was just testing you. To see if you've learned something!"

Soon I became accustomed to his usual omissions, and I checked the horse even more carefully when he brought it over. But today the size of his smile tells me he is cooking up something special. Too bad, because today I'm not in the mood for any of his jokes.

The game is about to start, and my sexy biker hasn't shown up yet. I call him *sexy biker* because he rides a big black motorbike, and he usually dresses in leather biker clothes, even when he doesn't ride one. He was my physiotherapist for the long months in the winter when I was trying to regain the use of my wrist, the one I had surgery on and that still refuses to move fully. Fortunately, in polo one doesn't do a lot with the left hand. All the left hand is meant to do is to have enough strength to hold the reins. And for this, it was moving quite enough. After my doctor came to the conclusion that I needed a second operation, I stopped the weekly physio sessions, but I stayed in touch with him. We met for drinks once or twice, and I thought he looked pretty hot. I had no idea if this feeling was reciprocated, because he never said or did anything to let me know. We just had this in-between, friends-who-flirt type of thing going on, and the flirting wasn't really going anywhere. But yesterday he texted me to ask if I wanted to meet for a drink, and I told him I couldn't. I was playing a polo tournament, and I invited him to come over and watch.

I might come he replied. *I'll see in the morning. Send me the address please.*

It was a weak answer, but I didn't mind. It was better than nothing. I sent him the address and patiently waited for him to show up. But it was almost time to get on the horse, and there was no sight of my sexy biker.

"Come on, Pedrito! Hurry up. I need to get going, the other players are on their horses already!" I try to cut Pedrito's jokes short. But he isn't having any of it.

"Here's your horse, Rosanna. Ready to play!" His smile widens.

Ready my ass! I want to scream back. The *sopra-cincha*—the extra leather belt that keeps the saddle in place—is unbuckled, the headstall is open on one side, and the martingale flaps loose. To complete the picture, one of the leg bandages has started to come off.

"For God's sake, Pedrito! I haven't got time for all this!" I mutter again.

"Time for what? The horse is perfect." His smile hasn't left him for a second.

One by one I point out all the mistakes to him. His smile is so wide that I think he's going to swallow both me and the horse. The wider his smile, the greater my irritation. I really need to get on a horse soon. My teammates are out of sight, already crossing the small bushes that separate the pony lines from the polo field.

"Very well, Rosanna! Today was the last test. You noticed everything. There's nothing more I can teach you."

I hope these jokes will come to an end now, I think as I patiently wait for Pedrito to remedy the disasters.

In the next three minutes I'm finally on the horse—it turns out that Pedrito is as fast as he is cheeky. I grip my mallet and get the horse into a canter towards the polo field, but I'm stopped by a horrible loud noise accompanied by someone calling my name.

It's him, the sexy biker! He's arrived at the last minute on his wild motorbike. A rush of excitement washes over me, but I can't savor this unexpected moment of happiness because I'm late on the field, and the sound of his bike makes the horses nervous.

"Shut the engine off, for God's sake! The horses will go wild soon. And come watch, the field is over there, through these bushes." I point with my mallet. "I need to go now," I add. "My team is already on the field."

"Good luck!" I hear, with no motorbike engine this time, just as I break into a canter again. I haven't told him that I'm happy to see him, it occurs to me as I gallop across the field to take my place next to my teammates. And I really am very happy to see him. It's the first time a guy has come to watch me play. I've managed to bring a couple of non-polo-playing girlfriends so far, but never a guy. Maybe this is the proof he's really into me.

And maybe today is the day when the friendly flirting will rise to the next level, another cheerful thought comes and settles in my mind.

On the field, my teammates are already lined up. Thank God the other team is spread all over the place, because otherwise I would have been the last one on the field, and that is really not a good place to be. I would have been shouted at by the Old Man again, no doubt. He's playing with us as the professional, and Jonny is playing as the professional of the other team. I find it hard to play against Jonny, but such are tournaments at this club, you rarely choose which team you play on.

Playing with the Old Man has its advantages, though. Sometimes he makes miracles happen, and then we'll win, I think as I'm taking my place lining up as number one, the weakest position in the team. I long ago have given up being bothered by my usual number one position. In polo the order of the pack becomes clear very soon. And no one disputes it. Everyone else on my team is much better than I am, that's a fact. I know it and they know it too. So there's no point being bothered.

Out of the corner of my eye, I notice my sexy biker walking along the side of the field and slowly approaching the middle of the field where the other people are gathered to watch the game. He walks inside the safety zone, blissfully unaware that this narrow strip of about ten feet is play territory and reserved for the players at all times, even if it's outside the boards. The umpire will not let the game start if any bystander is inside the safety zone.

Sure enough, the umpire and the rest of us wait until my sexy biker arrives at the center and is told by some friendly spectator to sit and watch outside the safety zone.

I'm feeling a little bit embarrassed by the lack of polo knowledge displayed by my potential date, but I have no time to dwell on it because the ball has left the umpire's hand, and the familiar scream fills my ears once more:

"Plaaaay!"

I spur my horse into immediate action because I want to play well when sexy biker is watching me. I get the ball soon and then glance towards the spectators to see if sexy biker sees me with the ball, and I can't tell because it's too far. In the meantime I lose it because it only takes a second of letting one's eyes off the ball for an adversary to steal it.

Then I try again, but no chance this time; the game has moved somewhere in the distance, and I try to catch up with them, galloping on Sorpresa, thinking about Pedrito and his jokes and whether all his tack-testing mistakes have been remedied.

"Rosannaaa! What were you doing last night?" I hear his shout across the polo field.

Oh, shut up, please. Don't embarrass me! The Old Man likes to do this sometimes, and when he starts, there's no way to stop him.

I am trying to hurry up since I guess what bothers him is my lack of adequate speed, but the shout comes again, within earshot of all my teammates.

"Rosannna! What were you doing last night?"

My blood comes up into my cheeks, but I carry on riding fast, trying to get away from him and his comments.

"Drinking? Partying? Not possible to play so bad if no drinking last night, Rosannaaaaa!"

I don't know if this is because I'm too slow or I'm losing the ball, but it doesn't matter. I wish he would shut up. I wonder if he's picking on me because he noticed that sexy biker has come to watch me. He is like this, the Old Man, he likes making jokes with his players, especially when there's a potential romantic connection within earshot. And he sees everything. On or off the polo field.

A ball hits me in the head. Thank God it was me and not the horse; at least I have a helmet. But the Old Man has his eyes on me, and I suffer one more comment about being asleep on the horse, which influences the quality of my playing today, or rather the lack of it.

Every time we go close to the spectators, I wonder if sexy biker is watching me and if I look good enough in the saddle. Is my back arched tall enough? Does my bum look too big? I know I should be thinking about the game, but I just can't stop thinking about my sexy biker.

Then we stop because there is a fault, and the other team has a penalty to take, and the Old Man gives me even more grief.

"Wake up, Rosanna! Wake up!"

Yes, all right, I will. Please pick on someone else, I think as I take my place next to the guy from the other team I'm supposed to mark. I make sure I'm on his stick side, otherwise I'll get more annoying comments from the Old Man.

The other team hits, and all of a sudden the ball is in front of me. I will hit! This is my hit and we're even close enough to the sidelines that sexy biker can see it properly. A quick thought flashes through my mind. I read in a polo book that I should visualize the word SLOW just before I hit the ball, no matter how fast I go. I try to do it but instead I see the word STILL. All of a sudden everything around me becomes still, and the horse galloping under me is no longer there. The wind blowing through my nostrils has stopped, my mallet slowly rises up behind me, and I am contained inside a bubble of stillness. For a fraction of a second, I breathe this stillness in deeply as the head of my mallet falls behind me, then follows through, and somehow miraculously finds the ball. Shot!

"*Buena!*" shouts the Old Man. He's as generous with his praise as he is with his critiques.

I rise high up in the stirrups as the horse continues galloping like mad, and I feel light as a feather. And good. I feel really good, good like I've only ever experienced after a good polo shot. I can only hope the sexy biker has seen it.

I ride fast, as fast as I can, hoping to hit it again, but Jonny, playing for the other team, is even faster, and he gets the ball now and he's turning it nicely in circles, *click click click,* just as he taught me to do during our countless stick-and-ball lessons. I'm trying to catch him up and attempt to win the ball back, even though I clearly know I stand no chance, but my horse doesn't want to listen; the mad gallop has got her adrenaline up, and she runs like a wild beast all the way to the other side of the field.

"Rosanna-a-a-a! What are you doing with that horse so far away?" The Old Man doesn't miss any of my moves today.

"She doesn't want to listen!" I shout back, irritated. "What can I do?"

He's too far away to answer, but a few minutes later, in the break between the chukkas I get my answer. The Old Man rides up to me and asks me a straight question: "Why do you think you're carrying a whip?"

I'm not sure what he's up to, so I don't answer. I just take a quick glance at the whip I carry in my left hand, the same hand that holds all four reins.

"Tell me, Rosanna!" he insists. "Why do you carry the whip? For the picture at the end of the chukka? No, Rosanna, let me tell you; it's not for the picture. You can use it!"

There's not much for me to do except nod in agreement.

"Next time your horse wants to fly away, make sure you use it," he adds before he disappears back on the field mounted on his new horse.

My next horse is waiting, perfectly saddled this time. Pedrito must have understood that there's no time for jokes. It's Sorpresa, my darling Sorpresa. I love this horse. I wouldn't be able to use the whip on her if she decided to fly with me to the end of the county!

I take a glimpse towards the sidelines where the sexy biker is sitting on the grass chatting to another girl. I feel a stab of jealousy, but I know the girl—she's the girlfriend of one of my teammates—so it's all right, I tell myself.

We get back on the field for the next chukka, and then something happens. Just like all the unexpected things that happen in polo, in one unfortunate second, reality as you know it is no longer there. In full gallop, Sorpresa trips, falls down on her knees, and I fly out of the saddle. I fly far above the horse's head and land perfectly on my elbows some ten feet in front of her. Thank God I have my elbow protectors on is the only thought I can register.

I hear the whistle, and the game stops. The game always stops when a player is thrown out of the saddle. I stand up immediately, dizzy, expecting pain somewhere in my body. Another bone maybe? I must have broken something. This type of fall was exactly like the one I had last year. There must be something seriously wrong with me. Again.

But no, there doesn't seem to be anything. The other players gather around me, and Jonny dismounts immediately.

"Are you OK?"

I seem to be fine. I walk a few steps, rotate my arms, my elbows. I don't feel pain. I can't believe I don't feel any pain. I wonder if it's possible to break something and not feel any pain.

"She's fine!" The Old Man gives the verdict to the umpire. "Check the horse," he adds, looking at Jonny. In polo, the next priority after a player's well-being is the well-being of the horse. Jonny runs in a circle holding Sorpresa by the reins to show the umpire that the horse is fine too. She trots perfectly; there's nothing wrong with her. And as unbelievable as it may seem, there's nothing wrong with me either.

"You're fine, Roxana. It's only a fall." Jonny is holding the horse for me to remount. "You're fine!" he repeats, stronger this time, as if he sees on my face that I'm having a hard time believing him.

I'm fine, it suddenly hits me. A bit shaken but I'm fine. I even forget about the sexy biker as I get back in the saddle. All I can think of is that a miracle has just happened: I took a fall and broke nothing.

The game carries on, and I ride a little slower this time, but I don't get any more shouts from the Old Man. He probably thinks it's safer not to push me.

In the end, we win. It's been a good game, and the Old Man played his usual tricks on the less experienced players of the other team to win the ball, and then he scored the winning goal with one long straight shot from a sixty-yard penalty. Only the Old Man can do this.

As we shake hands at the end of the game, I bring my horse next to his and say, "I need to ask you something. My fall? What happened? How come I fell like this? Did I do something wrong?"

I can't read his face. His eyes are hidden under the goggles, and he doesn't smile. He keeps silent, waiting for his horse to take a few steps as if what he's about to say needs to be thought through, and then he finally says in a nostalgic tone, "You know, Rosanna… when I was young, I was dating many girls."

I pull the horse to a stop, unsure where he's going with this. Maybe he's now going to make fun of my sexy biker and totally ignore my serious question.

"Many girls, Rosanna… and you know what?" He's now stopped his horse at my side "Once I decided to break up with one, I did so. I just broke up. I didn't want to see her anymore; I didn't want to think about her. She was gone from my mind, as if she never were. Done. Gone."

"Yes?" I ask, still unsure what all this had to do with my fall.

"It's the same with your fall," he says, his face still serious. "It happened. And it's done. You shouldn't think about it. I don't want to talk about it. It's gone. Like it's never been."

And with a sharp move he breaks into a canter and rides away from me.

"James!" He shouts to another player.

"James! I told you, son, how many times did I tell you? No sleeping with girlfriend before a tournament! Look at you, out of breath and almost falling out of the saddle! What can I do if you don't want to listen? Next time, no sleeping with girlfriend before tournament! Please!"

Poor guy, his girlfriend came up to congratulate him at the end of the game and heard this friendly advice for sure.

I give up trying to find answers to unanswerable questions and find Pedrito so I can hand over my horse. I jump off, throw him the reins, take my bottle of water in exchange, and hurry off to find my sexy biker. There's always a barbecue after the game, and we'll sit down and talk and maybe see where all this flirting business goes.

But sexy biker is already on his motorbike. He tells me he enjoyed watching the game and he hopes I'm feeling all right after the nasty fall I took. Otherwise I will have to come back for more physio sessions. Then he tells me he has to go because he's got some other things to do back in London, and he can't stay for the barbecue. But he thanks me for the invite to come watch a very interesting game.

"See you soon!" he adds, just before he puts his helmet on. And then he disappears with a roar in a cloud of dust. Like the Old Man would say: gone. Like he's never been.

I'm disappointed but too tired to make a big drama out of his departure. Well, at least he showed up. It's better than nothing, I try to convince myself.

I sit and eat with my teammates in my dirty white jeans, because I still didn't remember to bring another pair to change into. I sit next to the Old Man, who pours some lemonade into my wine and tells me it's a better way to drink it. I sit there surrounded by my polo family, and I'm not even too sad that sexy biker isn't there.

I'm not alone, after all.

Blood, Pains, and Gains

AUGUST

It's been a painful game so far. I don't know why, some games are just like this. They hurt. I got a ball in the back, and it hurt too. It will probably leave a big black bruise under my shoulder blade. At least I won't be able to see it, unlike the bruises on my legs that refuse to fade and make me want to cover up my legs, even though it's summer and I could wear a miniskirt. But one does not wear a miniskirt with legs bruised from polo ride-offs.

Think of the game, I tell myself as I come to the pony lines to change horses. The ball, the score, the teammates. It's the second chukka, we have two more to go. Forget about the bruise, just forget about it.

But then Sorpresa is hit by a ball. I feel her jerk, and I feel her pain stabbing my heart. It's OK, I try to tell myself. It's just a ball. It will pass. She's a big horse. And unlike me, she will not be left with a bruise. Or maybe she will, under her short, shiny coat of brown hair, but no one will be able to see it.

And then Jonny is hit as he leans out of the saddle to pick up a ball. He's good at leaning out of the saddle, Jonny. Unlike me, his knees don't give in that easily. Another player from the other team attempted to hit the same ball, and the mallet came up and hit Jonny in the face. He doesn't wear a face guard. None of the professionals wear face guards. I don't wear one either, but it's because I can't stand the feeling of claustrophobia as I look out on the field between the bars.

"Jonny, are you OK?" I shout, and ride towards him.

"Sorry!" the guy from the other team shouts. "I didn't see you!"

There's nothing to be sorry about; polo is like this. We swing and we hit. It's our own responsibility to stay out of someone else's hit.

The umpire blows the whistle because Jonny is now holding his head with his right arm, the mallet hanging inert off the hook around his thumb.

"Jonny-y-y-y!" I still shout even though I'm next to him by now. "What happened? Are you OK?"

He lifts his head and I can see blood around his mouth. I wonder what he's broken. Teeth? Some players play with mouth guards, but not many. It's impossible to shout wearing a mouth guard, and one cannot be captain of a team and not shout at the other players.

"*Nada*," he says. "It's nothing."

"What do you mean *nada*? Jonny!! You're bleeding… we need to stop the game!"

I don't know why this happens, but I can feel the pain of others more than I feel my own. The mare, now Jonny's. The other two players on our team gather around. But Jonny doesn't want any fuss.

He wipes his mouth clean with his gloved hand, spits the blood out, and mumbles, "*Nada*. Just a little bit of blood. *Sangre*. We continue!"

"But, Jonny!" I plead even though I don't really know what I'm pleading for. He can't stop the game and there's no one to replace him with. He is the captain of the team. Of course he needs to carry on playing.

"*Vamooos*! Let's go!" he shouts as his horse breaks into a canter. "We have a game to win!"

We line up for a throw-in. We don't get a penalty; it wasn't a fault this time. When a player is hit, it's not necessarily a fault in polo. I line up next to him and I know I'm being ridiculous, but I just can't help asking one more time:

"Are you sure you're all right to play?"

He doesn't answer. Because of the blood in his mouth most probably.

"He just won't be able to kiss any girls for a while!" one of the other guys says, and they all laugh, and Jonny smiles too. A bloody smile.

"Line up!" I hear the shout of the umpire and then I decide to shut up and not ask anything any longer. I'm the only girl on the field today. I'm not going to make a fool of myself by getting so worried about a few drops of blood.

We won. We won the tournament! We took pictures with the cup, and then we passed it from one to the other; all four of us got to hold it, to treasure it. It's been a long and difficult fight. But we won.

I don't even register the weakness in my knees. I'll worry about it later, when I get home. Later. Not now. We are celebrating now.

"Here! You hold it!" I say as I turn to the guy on my right and pass the cup to him. He's played as number three. It's a strong position, usually the strongest in the team. But in this case the strongest position was Jonny's and he liked playing as number four. So number three was the second strongest position in this game.

He takes the cup and then I see his hands. The left one, the one he held the reins with. I see the deep cut that runs through two of his fingers and the clogged blood all around it.

"What happened to your hand?" I ask, my voice rising with alarm.

"Nothing; it's nothing," he insists.

Men like this word. Nothing. It never means nothing.

I grab his hand and turn it palm up to have a better look.

"You need to put something on it; this cut… it's deep. What happened?"

He doesn't say it, but I know. The reins most probably. Holding the reins of a horse that doesn't want to stop, and holding them without a glove.

"You played without gloves?"

He nods. It's obvious, no need to deny it.

"Why?"

"Because I was late. You guys were already on the field. I didn't want to make you wait."

I nod too. Of course he wouldn't. An umpire could decide to start the game anyway, even if one team was incomplete. The most important duty a player has is to show up. On the field, next to his teammates. You always show up, no matter what. You don't let your teammates down, you just don't.

In his case it meant he had no time to look for his gloves. Not while an umpire asks his teammates to line up for the initial throw-in of the game. And he played without them. It wasn't a mandatory piece of equipment after all.

There's nothing else to ask, nothing else to say. The cut will heal. And we won the game.

They gave me the cup to take home that day. It was nice of them because I was the least experienced player in the team, and I really didn't contribute that much to the victory. But they said I'd never had a cup at home, and I should enjoy the feeling. I'd keep it for a year and then I'd return it to the club so that a new tournament would be played for this cup, and it would be passed on again to the winning team. But now I had my name engraved on it together with those of my teammates. The winning team.

I get home late that evening, place the cup in my living room on top of my mantel, and look at it once more, my heart beaming.

I forget about stretching, it's too late anyway. I toss my dirty white jeans in a corner, gulp down a protein shake as a replacement for dinner, and go straight to bed. I'm tired and sore, and I need some sleep. I desperately need some sleep. Tomorrow's Monday and I need to go to work, I have a big presentation to do. But tomorrow is still a world away. I fall asleep, still holding that cup in my dreams.

The Game of Kings

SEPTEMBER

There are only a few games left this season, I think as I drive my car onto the field next to the pony lines. We always park there, one car after the other until the entire grassy patch is filled with cars and players. We get ready for the game by the cars, putting on various bits of equipment and throwing clothes and shoes onto the back seats. A polo player's car is usually in a perpetual state of mess.

It will be an easy game today, I think as I switch the engine off. I will mark Kate, who's my perfect player to mark. She's my friend and about the same level as me in polo. Whenever possible, the Old Man tries to put us in opposing teams during tournaments so we can mark each other. It's always a pleasure to mark her. We have a sort of ladies' agreement not to be rough with each other, so there's no pushing, no ride-off, and no battling for the ball. We let the rest of the guys do all that. Instead, we sometimes talk while we ride together in the middle of the game, as if that's the perfect opportunity for a catch-up. Don't get me wrong, we play to win, but it's nice to play against her, especially because the player you're supposed to mark from the other team is the player you're likely to spend most of the game near.

Kate has arrived already; I spot her car closer to the horses. She drives a Mini, just like me. There must be something about Minis and girls in polo. She runs to say hi as she spots me, and tells me, all excited, that the new handicaps for the end of the season have been published.

"Already?" I ask, surprised, my heart racing with hope.

The handicap is a big thing in polo. It reflects the level of the player, and it's reviewed annually at the end of the season. When you start playing, once you pass the rules test and the head of the club decides you are safe enough on the field, you get a handicap of -2. That's the pure beginner's level. Saying that, it takes a long time, usually about a year to get to -2. After this it's up to you. If your game improves by the end of the season your handicap might go up to reflect this. You might become a -1 or even a 0. A 0 handicap is usually a very good player. Only a few amateurs make it to 1. And only professionals have a handicap of 2 and above. As there are only a few levels you can attain as a non-professional, it's a big deal when your handicap is put up. Some people, like Kate, for instance, absolutely do not want their handicap increased. That's because if your handicap goes up, so does the pressure. If you're a -1 you're expected to play as a -1. You're no longer the beginner of the team and your mistakes are no longer tolerated. There will be someone else with a -2 handicap coming up to take your place. Your handicap is added up to that of the rest of the team, and if there are handicap differences with the team you're playing against, they might get free goals. So there's pressure for any player who's not a total beginner to play up to the handicap they've been awarded. It's a serious business. Games can be lost or won on handicap merits alone.

But, on the other hand, if you're an ambitious player who pours his or her heart and soul into the game, like I am, then having your handicap rise at the end of the season becomes the ultimate reward.

It's like a medal or public recognition for how much you've improved your game. This is how I viewed it, and I hoped—I desperately prayed—that my handicap would increase.

"Yes, they've already been published. Isn't that great?" Kate confirms. "And mine remains unchanged! No pressure for the next season. Polo just the way I like to play it!" Her smile is wide, and I can feel her relief.

"And mine?" I ask, trying to keep my voice neutral.

"Unchanged," she replies, shattering all my hopes with one word. "Isn't that great? We can still go on to mark each other next season too."

If my handicap were to be increased, she would probably get another -2 player to mark. I can understand her excitement, but I don't share it. I actually feel like I might throw up. In the distance, I spot someone congratulating a guy whose handicap has been put up. He was a -2 just like me. Now he's a -1. Some guys are joking with him, telling him he's got to play up to his new level now. He pretends to be scared, but we all know he's happy. Of course he's happy. I would be too. I struggle hard to hold back my tears.

"Oh no!" Kate exclaims. We haven't spoken about this but my face must have shown all the disappointment I harbored inside. "You were hoping for a rise, weren't you? You know it's just an ego thing, right? It's much better to stay the same handicap. It's better to play above your level than below!"

Yes, I know. Whenever a player's handicap is raised, he or she will inevitably play a bit lower than the actual level of the handicap. But then they will catch up. Their game will most likely get better precisely because of the peer pressure. But with an unchanged handicap, no one expects you to play better than you did last year.

I nod silently and start taking my equipment out of the car. The game is about to start, and no one cares about my hidden disappointment. Plus, the Old Man is within earshot, and I really don't want to discuss my handicap or my disappointment with him.

I throw him a quick glance. He appears not to have heard our conversation. He is busy holding the reins of a horse for a new guy to mount. I've seen this guy a few times on the training field, and he's not yet ready to play in a tournament. He's a true beginner, not even a -2. He'll most likely take his horse onto the stick-and-ball field and practice some more shots. That is, if he manages to get on the horse at all, because I notice he seems to be fiddling a lot with the stirrups as if he can't decide whether to put them up or down. The Old Man watches him with that amused expression on his face I know so well. He's about to say something; I can feel it in the air.

And, sure enough, he does. Just as the new guy sticks his foot into the stirrups and tries to lift himself into the saddle, I hear the Old Man shouting, "Sto-o-op!"

The Old Man has an unmistakable shout. It seems more like a scream, and it's loud enough to be heard above the heavy noise of eight horses hitting the ground in full gallop. Wherever you are on the polo field, you are guaranteed to hear the Old Man when he shouts. And there are no horses running around here, so every single one of us hears his shout.

The new guy freezes, one leg lifted and his foot inserted in the stirrup, one hand on the saddle and another one holding his mallet. He just freezes here unsure what to do next. He can't seem to decide whether to go up or back.

The Old Man's shouts are like that. They always achieve their purpose. We're now all listening carefully, anticipating a show. Only the poor new guy has no idea what's in store for him.

"Tell me one thing!" the Old Man continues, feeling confident he now has everybody's attention.

The guy nods, incapable of articulating anything.

"Are you married?"

Oh no. I wish I could see his face. He probably didn't anticipate this. No one could ever anticipate the questions of the Old Man when he puts his mind to it.

"Tell me!" He screams again. "Are you married?"

"No," the guy says in a low voice. He finally pulls his leg out of the stirrup and places it on the ground. He seems very unsure of what he should do next.

"Have you got a girlfriend?" The Old Man continues the questioning.

"No," the guy repeats.

I see a few amused faces. We're already very familiar with the Old Man's methods and are enjoying the show.

"Very good." The Old Man nods approvingly. "Very very good. You know why?"

There's no answer this time. The guy just watches him with a face that says it all. He suspects the Old Man has gone crazy.

"Let me tell you why," says the Old Man, patiently. "Look around you!" he points out to all of us, with one large gesture. "There are so many lovely girls playing polo here! Rosanna, for instance." He now points directly at me. "Single. Or Kate, here." He doesn't even look around to locate her. His arm finds her automatically.

"Single too. Or Daniela, there by the other car. So many nice girls here who are single. Do you want them to see you getting on the horse like that?"

The cheeks of the new guy start burning. Mine too but for a different reason.

"Never get on the horse without holding the reins. Hear me? Never! Remember this!" the Old Man concludes with a serious face handing over the reins to the new guy.

I bet he will never forget this lesson.

As for me, I swallow my sorrow and fasten the strap of the helmet under my chin, feeling grateful that my goggles are covering my eyes and no one can read the sadness in them. I'm single and with no change of handicap either. And I've just been publicly identified as both.

What a great achievement for the end of the season!

The game starts shortly afterwards and I try hard to play well. If I were a real polo player, I should be able to manage my emotions and not let them play on my mind. But I fail. The sorrow in me builds its way up to the surface, and I miss the ball, I misread the game, I get shouted at by the Old Man, and I get asked by my teammates what is wrong with me. I can't tell them that I have no idea, but something is seriously wrong with me. I haven't had my handicap increased, and I'm still single.

In the last chukka, my team is awarded a great penalty shot. A true stroke of luck. It's a free hit from the spot or a hundred feet from the goalpost, we can choose which one, and in this case we choose the spot because the foul occurred some two feet away from the goalpost. We have one shot, only one shot, but the ball is so close to the goal that it's almost impossible to miss.

"Rosanna!" the Old Man shouts again. Why does everyone always shout on a polo field, even when there's no need?

"You take it!"

Why should I take it? I wasn't the one who got fouled. It's normally the guy against whom the foul happened who takes the free shot. But no, this time the Old Man insists it be me. I guess he's trying to encourage me after my disastrous play.

"Come on, Rosanna, you do it. You can't miss this. You can't possibly miss this one. I am gifting you this goal, to get you back on track. Let's see how you score!"

And then I miss. I miss because I swing badly, and a bad swing creates a bad hit, and the ball goes astray to the astonishment of everyone present, including myself.

"Noooo!" the Old Man screams.

"This is not possible, Rosanna! Not possible," he repeats. "Even if you wanted to miss it, you couldn't have done it! That shot was like mini-golf. All you had to do was touch the ball!"

We ride back to the center of the field to line up for our last throw-in of the game, and I don't answer. No one else asks me anything. I guess they don't expect anything better from a -2 player whose handicap hasn't been raised.

But after the game, the Old Man comes to find me. We've lost. As soon as the umpire blows his whistle, I jump off the horse, hand the reins to Pedrito, throw my equipment in the car, and decide to leave early. I don't want to hang around and let the others see my sadness. Everyone else is still on the field getting ready to enjoy the barbecue and a drink while debating the best moments of the game. I just disappear and run away without saying a word. I go straight to the tack room to leave my mallets and boots and try to hurry out and hide in the car before the tears I've been holding back since the beginning of the game find a way out

"Rosanna!" The Old Man has found me. "What's happening with you?"

I don't answer. But I don't need to. He already knows.

"It's the handicap, isn't it?" he asks, his eyes piercing my face. You're upset your handicap hasn't been increased, is that right?"

There's no point denying it. Nothing can escape his sharp eyes anyway.

"Listen to me, Rosanna. I am doing you a favor by not putting your handicap up. Do you hear me? Your game is not yet of a -1 level. It's not. That's how things are. It's almost there but not quite. You need to train more. Come with me to Argentina this winter. I'll make you a -1 handicap. Seriously."

I don't answer. Tears I can't stop any longer flood my eyes.

"Stop feeling so hurt by this stupid thing. The handicap. It doesn't matter. It's just silly. Completely silly. I'm doing you a favor," he repeats as if to justify himself.

I still don't answer, so he turns around to leave me to my misery. But before he does, he's got one more piece of wisdom for me:

"And stop caring so much about polo. Get a life. Get a boyfriend. Be happy. Don't use this sport to create all the happiness in your life. It can't. It's just a hobby."

With these parting words, he finally goes, but I stay there a long time. I sit on the bench under the row of nicely aligned mallets, all bearing the initials of the players. I stay there staring aimlessly at the many polo boots that wait to be polished, once the grooms are done with cleaning the horse tacks. I stay there and cry.

A rhyme comes into my mind as if to give me courage. It's from an inscription that has been found in today's Pakistan, the birthplace of polo. It's more than two thousand years old, engraved in stone. It says:

Let others play at other things
The king of games is still the game of kings.
Or queens, I add silently.

No one will see me cry over this again. After all, queens don't really cry. And there's no reason to cry, after all. Handicap increase or not, I've still got polo.

Student No More

OCTOBER

The polo season ended, and all that was left was the end-of-the-season party, usually held at an Argentine restaurant in central London. It was a big event. Every member of the club, professional player or groom, would be present. There would be speeches and awards and more opportunities for recognition. The handicap business was over, at least for this season, and I tried hard to put it out of my mind. But there would be a number of other prizes awarded during the end-of-the-season party and I was hoping that at least I would get a mention there. A little something, anything to make me feel noticed.

I put a lot into polo this summer, playing almost every tournament at the club. I played club chukkas during the week and trained on the stick-and-ball field under Jonny's relentless supervision every week. He told me my game had improved dramatically this season, and some other players thought so too. I know because they all told me. It appears everyone felt one way or the other that I had been disappointed with the handicap results and wanted to be supportive.

On the night of the polo party, I hide my sadness under pretty make-up. I put on a sexy dress and head over to the Argentine restaurant, determined to have a good night. We might go dancing after dinner and, who knows, I might even meet someone.

My summer had been as bare in the love chapter as it gets. My sexy biker had disappeared after coming to watch me play, and I wondered more than once if it was seeing me play polo that actually put him off. Or maybe the fall I took that day. And there was no one else, either on the field or off it. But there had been very few occasions where I could have met someone off the polo field this summer.

The party starts well. Everyone gets one prize or another, and everyone's merits are discussed and mentioned by the Old Man in his end-of-the-season speech. Everyone gets a small cup or medal or prize of some kind. Something to remind them of the great season we all had.

Someone gets the price for the best nearside shots. Another guy for being the fastest player on the field. Kate gets mentioned for the kind way in which she treats her ponies. Someone else gets the prize for the shiniest polo boots, and another guy gets mentioned for always being lucky and finding himself with the ball on the field through no effort of his own. Everyone gets something. And I get something too.

I get the prize for the best polo student of the season. The best polo student!

In his speech, the Old Man mentions me as the one who has tried the most to improve her game. Not that she actually has, because someone else gets the prize for the most improved player. No, I get the mention for trying hard. The best polo student of the season.

I'm handed a cup on which I see the words engraved. I swallow hard, and for a second I think that maybe it's a joke, and my true prize still awaits me. But no, it's real. I feel like I'm being told I tried hard but didn't get anywhere. My handicap is still the same. And my single status is unchanged as well.

Towards the end of the evening and many drinks later, I start seeing the funny side to this. The Universe has some unusual ways of delivering its messages, but I must say it's pretty effective this time. I get it. I will try no more. I will simply do. I will go to Argentina and train with the Old Man. I will train as much as I need to come back a -1-level player. And then all they can do is to raise my handicap next season.

I tell Kate, who is sitting next to me, about my plan.

"Maybe you're supposed to try less, not more!" She suggests a different perspective. "Maybe all you need to do is just chill, relax, and everything will come. The boyfriend, the handicap… all of it."

I tell her I'm determined to do it right this time. In my mind it all starts to take shape: I have surgery scheduled in two weeks, the surgery I've been postponing since the beginning of the season. My left wrist did its job this season; it doesn't hurt but it doesn't bend either. I'll have the surgery, and then I'll go to Argentina, I decide.

And then there's a bonus if I go: the Argentine men. Everyone says they are sexy, fun and attentive. And they make you feel like a queen. I feel my hopes rising. I might even meet someone there. And if not, there's always polo.

In the background I hear the Argentine music and people laughing, Jonny's voice mixing with that of the Old Man and other players talking to the grooms. One big happy family. My family. I take another sip of wine and feel my tense muscles relaxing. I don't even remember the silly prize any longer.

Yes, I will go back to Argentina, and I'll do it right this time. I know I will.

Running with Horses

OCTOBER

It's always cold in surgery rooms. I remember it well from last time. The only thing that's worse than the cold before the surgery, when you are kindly invited to lie down on the icy metal table, is the cold you feel afterwards when you wake up. I remember last time I shook for what seemed like an eternity.

Don't think about this, focus on the present, I tell myself. A kind voice to my right asks me to make a fist and release slowly. A needle is inserted into my vein, and I don't even feel it. Maybe it will be better this time, I try to encourage myself. It has to be. It's only a small bone in my wrist that needs to be broken again and put straight. No big deal. Not like last time. Surely not.

I hear them chatting, the nurses and the anesthesiologist and someone else. I can't see her as she's behind me. I can't see my doctor either, but he'll probably come in only once I'm asleep.

"You'll feel something warm in your vein now." I hear the kind voice again. I'm grateful for this. I'm too cold and too scared, and all I need right now is to be knocked unconscious.

I feel dizzy all of a sudden, as if I can't really remember why I'm here, what happened and what is going to happen. I'm very heavy and my mind is heavy too. Everything slows down.

Horses. Ah, yes. It was all about the horses. I think it has to do with horses. Why I'm here, I'm not sure. Actually… hang on… I want to ask the kind voice, but I can't hear it any longer, and I can't see much either because there's a bright light in my eyes coming from somewhere in the ceiling, and in this light I start seeing the horses. They've come for me. One after the other, they come through the light and surround me, and then I let go finally, and I feel like I'm falling into an abyss, and I become them and they become me. And together we start running as a herd, like horses do. We run through forests and meadows crossing rivers and valleys. The space stretches empty before us and we run and run. I run with them. I am them.

"Do you hear me?"

I run… with them. Horses. I've been running… running in the meadows.

"Do you hear me? Open your eyes. Wake up. Wake up!" repeats the voice.

And I fall back from the light. I feel I fall down again, and the horses melt around me. It all lasted a lifetime and no time at all.

"Very good! Now open your eyes. Your surgery is done. Everything went perfectly well. All you need to do is rest. And you'll be all right."

I'll be all right, my sleepy mind registers. They said so, too. They said I'll be just fine.

The horses.

Epilogue

The good thing about surgery is that you don't remember much afterwards. Pretty much like childbirth, I've been told. I have no idea what childbirth is like; I've never been through it. But I did go through surgery, and I'm very grateful my memory has been wiped out.

How can you want to play polo again after three broken bones and two operations? I was asked this by my family and non-polo-playing friends as soon as I got out of the hospital. I told them that it wasn't that bad and that I was going to recover soon. And no, it wasn't an exaggeration. It really wasn't that bad. All I remembered was running with the horses for what seemed like an eternity.

The thing that was really bad, though, was going to the hospital alone and then coming back home alone. No boyfriend, no one to hold me as I felt in pain. My polo buddies were gone. The season had ended, and we didn't normally keep in touch outside the season. The Old Man had called and offered to come to the hospital, but I told him there was no need, so he didn't come. My family would have come too, but they live far away in another country, and frankly I didn't feel like having them there either. They would simply have told me to give up polo.

So I went in alone, came home alone, and lay in bed for a few days with my left arm covered once again with huge bandages.

It was during those days that I booked it. My ticket to Argentina. A couple of weeks would be all I'd need for the initial recovery, so the stitches would be out, and I could travel safely. And then I'd go. A new chapter will start for me in Argentina.

I will recover my wrist.

I will find Mr. Right.

I will play polo.

And I will never fall again.

Mallorca, December 2018

Acknowledgments

As a polo player, I'm the sum of all the people who have taught me. Their grip on the reins has become mine; the way they hold their mallets has become my own. I learned my swing by copying theirs, and raised in half seat while watching them do so. Their passion for this game now runs through my own veins, their victories are mine, and mine are theirs. When I play, they play with me; in my every move and every breath, I am the sum of all of them. And when I ride my horse on a polo field, their words still ring in my ears:

"Rosanna, wake up, you are e-sleeping on the horse."—Carlito

"Go to the goal!"—Cholo

"Knees in, heels down."—Andrew

"Think like a horse." —Eddie

"Keep your shoulders back! Be proud to play polo!" —Jake

"Faster! I said faster!"—Jonny

"Let's go ride! The horses are ready." —Patricio

and many, many more…

My gratitude to you all.

About the Author

Roxana Valea was born in Romania and lived in Italy, Switzerland, England, and Argentina before settling in Spain. She has a BA in journalism and an MBA degree. She spent more than twenty years in the business world as an entrepreneur, manager and management consultant working for top companies such as Apple, eBay, and Sony. She is also a Reiki Master and shamanic energy medicine practitioner.

As an author, Roxana writes books inspired by real events. Her memoir *Through Dust and Dreams* is a faithful account of a trip she took at the age of twenty-eight across Africa by car in the company of two strangers she met over the internet. Her following book, *Personal Power: Mindfulness Techniques for the Corporate World* is a non-fiction book filled with personal anecdotes from her consulting years. The Polo Diaries series is inspired by her experiences as a female polo player—traveling to Argentina, falling in love, and surviving the highs and lows of this dangerous sport.

Roxana lives with her husband in Mallorca, Spain, where she writes, coaches, and does energy therapies, but her first passion remains writing.

www.roxanavalea.com

A Horse Called Bicycle, The Polo Diaries Book 2, 2020

Roxy found love . . . but is it enough?

In the second installment of the Polo Diaries series, polo player Roxy goes back to Argentina a year after the events in *Single in Buenos Aires*, filled with dreams of settling down with the man she loves. This time, once again, Argentina is full of surprises and things are not what they appear to be. Or maybe they're exactly what they're meant to be, as a fortune-teller informs her.

Roxy takes a leap of faith and follows her dreams once again. She spends time at glamorous party venues of Buenos Aires and travels to the rough and wild pampas. Along the way, Roxy's friends support and champion her quest for love, but when things get out of hand, Roxy realizes she needs to listen to her own inner voice and must make a hard choice. Two paths open in front of her, each one with far-reaching consequences. Which will she choose?

Other Books by Roxana Valea

Through Dust and Dreams, 2014

At a crossroads in her life, Roxana decides to take a ten-day safari trip to Africa. In Namibia, she meets a local guide who talks about "the courage to become who you are" and tells her that "the world belongs to those who dream."

Her holiday over, Roxana still carries the spell of his words within her soul. Six months later she quits her job and searches for a way to fulfil an old dream: crossing Africa from north to south. Teaming up with Richard and Peter, two total strangers she meets over the internet, Roxana starts a journey that will take her and her companions from Morocco to Namibia, crossing deserts and war-torn countries and surviving threats from corrupt officials and tensions within their own group.

Through Dust and Dreams is the story of their journey: a story of courage and friendship, of daring to ask questions and search for answers, and of self-discovery on a long, dusty road south.
www.throughdustanddreams.com

Personal Power: Mindfulness Techniques for the Corporate World, 2018

This book is about your power. The one you were born with, the power that is always in you waiting to be used. Blending concepts of psychology, mindfulness and practical spirituality with the author's twenty-plus years of experience in the corporate world, it presents a simple yet powerful seven-step framework to connect with your power and use it to manifest the life that you want.

You will learn to ground, cleanse and protect your energy. You will tap into what you already know and learn how to make decisions using your power base. You will be reminded how to direct your energy to manifest abundance and to reflect on and constantly improve your process.

If you want to achieve a sense of self-determination and inner peace while still working in a hectic corporate environment, and wonder how some people do this effortlessly, this book is for you.

www.personalpowercorporate.com

www.ingramcontent.com/pod-product-compliance
Lightning Source LLC
Chambersburg PA
CBHW021658110726
47902CB00007B/1982